Follow Andrina Adamo's dancing career through these
new editions of the Drina ballet books.

The Drina books:

1. Ballet for Drina
2. Drina's Dancing Year
3. Drina Dances in Exile
4. Drina Dances in Italy
5. Drina Dances Again
6. Drina Dances in New York
7. Drina Dances in Paris
8. Drina Dances in Madeira
9. Drina Dances in Switzerland
10. Drina Goes on Tour
11. Drina Ballerina

Drina Dances in Switzerland

by

Jean Estoril

SIMON & SCHUSTER
YOUNG BOOKS

Cover artwork by Kevin Jones
Cover design by Terence Kingston
Illustrations by Jenny Sanders

Text copyright © Jean Estoril 1964

First published in Great Britain by Hodder & Stoughton Ltd
Second edition published in Great Britain by MacDonald & Co
(Publishers) Ltd

This edition published in 1992 by
Simon & Schuster Young Books
Campus 400
Maylands Avenue
Hemel Hempstead HP2 7EZ

Printed and bound at Cox & Wyman Ltd, Reading, Berkshire,
England

British Library Cataloguing in Publication Data available

ISBN: 0-7500-1268-4

CONTENTS

BOOK ONE
Ballet all Alone

1

Drina's Grim Resolve

Drina was standing on Westminster Bridge waiting for her friend Rose Conway. It was a bright morning in late August and Big Ben had just struck ten-thirty. The traffic whirled past just behind her, but Drina, staring down at the grey river, was for once quite unaware of her surroundings. Usually she loved the London scene, especially when the weather was warm and sunny, but now she was completely absorbed in her unhappy thoughts.

Only the previous day she and her grandparents had returned from their holiday in Madeira and Drina's lovely suntan made her look darker and more foreign than usual. It had been a wonderful holiday in some ways, for she had adored Madeira and there had been the added thrill of dancing with the members of the Lingeraux Ballet Company, with whom she had made friends on the ship. But, towards the end of the time in Funchal, she had had bad news: news that had plunged her into despair all the deeper because her true feelings had had to be hidden from her grandfather. How *hard* it was to stick to her grim resolve and to try to pretend all the time that she was quite happy and looking forward to all the coming changes.

"Drina!" Rose arrived at her side with a rush. She lived at Earls Court and was, these days, Drina's closest friend. Jenny Pilgrim, who lived in the Warwickshire town of Willerbury, had once held first place in Drina's affections, but, sadly enough, they had grown apart during the past year or two. Drina minded greatly, feeling that it was partly her fault, but there was no doubt that Jenny had changed. For one thing Jenny had so many troubles of her own that Drina felt now that she could not burden her friend with her own problems.

"Oh, Rose, I *am* so glad to see you!"

"Me, too. I've been dying to see you again. You look simply wonderful!" Rose herself looked very pretty and was even quite sunburnt after her holiday with her family. Usually she was extremely pale, for she lived in a small, overcrowded house and was sometimes in trouble over her diet. Rose was going to be a very good dancer, but those in authority at the Dominick Ballet School were sometimes sorry that she was now too old to stay at the Residential School in the Chilterns, where she had lived for two years on a scholarship.

"I don't *feel* wonderful."

Rose immediately grew sober and studied her friend's face anxiously.

"What's the matter, Drina? You were so mysterious on the telephone. Is it really bad news? Your grandfather isn't ill again?"

"No, he's much better, but the news is partly to do with him. I couldn't say much on the phone. I thought Granny might be listening, and I knew you'd shriek the roof off if I tried to tell you then. Let's walk along the Embankment and sit in the gardens. I'll tell you first and

then I have to see Miss Volonaise at the Dominick
Theatre about eleven-thirty."

"Madam? Why?"

"Well, I telephoned her just now. Not from the flat –
from a public call-box. I rang her home first, but the
housekeeper said she was at the theatre. There's a full
rehearsal, because they're starting with the new
programme on Monday. I just had to talk to her, and
she said she had been hoping for the chance to speak to
me. We're to watch the rehearsal until she's ready."

"Can I come as well, then?" Though puzzled, and
growing more worried every minute, Rose could still
take pleasure in the thought of watching a Dominick
rehearsal.

"She said so. She knew I was meeting you."

"But why Madam? Is it as important as that?" Rose
was still overawed by Marianne Volonaise, one of the
directors of the Dominick Ballet Company and School.
Drina had once shared the feeling, in company with
most of the younger students, but circumstances had
changed all that during the past year or two. For one
thing Miss Volonaise now knew that Drina's mother
had been the great dancer, Elizabeth Ivory, once prima
ballerina of the company and also a personal friend of
both Marianne Volonaise and Igor Dominick. Drina had
wished to keep the fact a secret, for she had long ago
vowed that she would succeed as a dancer without the
impetus of her mother's name, and it was still a secret
from most people. But Mr Dominick and Miss
Volonaise had found out during the Edinburgh Festival
the previous August, when Drina had been there with
the Dominick Company, dancing Little Clara in *Casse
Noisette*.

Drina talked about Madeira and how she had danced
with the Lingeraux Company, until they were settled on

a seat in the gardens, but then Rose could bear it no longer.

"It all sounds marvellous and you were very lucky. But I can't wait another minute. Out with it!"

"I almost can't talk about it," Drina said, with obvious difficulty. "I feel so awful about the whole thing. Rose, I'm not going to be at the Dominick at all this winter. I'm –"

"Not at the Dominick?" Rose did indeed "shriek the roof off" and three holiday-makers on the next seat glanced across in surprise. "But you must be! Where are you going? I don't understand."

Drina said carefully:

"Grandfather has to spend the winter out of England and Granny said ... she almost *made* me ... I have to go with them. She says, and I know she's quite right, that Grandfather would only worry if they left me behind in London with Miss Whiteway. It would be bad for him, for he still isn't very strong. In fact, the doctor said that he might die if he stayed in England. He nearly died in the summer, as you know, and I thought then that, if he lived, I'd do anything in the world for him. I – I didn't know that I'd be put to the test so soon."

Rose was now completely silent. She gulped a few times and tossed back her brown hair, staring at the sparrows hopping fearlessly round her feet.

"It nearly killed me when I heard," Drina went on, remembering that hot and brilliant afternoon when she had dashed out of the Madeira hotel and climbed high into the mountains, facing her situation. "But I knew at once that I had to do it. I *had* to make Grandfather believe that I didn't mind. I'm not convinced, even now, that he really believes me, but I've done my best."

"But, Drina, where – where are you going?"

Drina sighed.

"Most girls would probably think it a wonderful chance. My grandparents have rented a furnished villa in the Ticino, the Italian part of Switzerland, near Lake Lugano. And my Italian cousin Antonia goes to a finishing school near there. I'm afraid it – it will finish *me* all right, but that's where I'm going. I'll spend the weekends at the villa."

"But – but what about your dancing?" Rose's voice was still breathless. The thought of a whole winter without Drina was dreadful to her, and also she knew well just what it would cost her friend to miss two terms at the Dominick.

"Oh, that's fixed. There's a visiting teacher from La Scala, Milan. She comes twice a week and I'm to have lessons alone with her. There's a studio and I shall be able to practise. But – but, of course, I shall be utterly cut off from the theatre, and I shall hate just dancing by myself –" Drina's voice shook, though she tried hard to keep it steady. "I shan't see any of you, and everything will go on without me, and when I come back the Dominick will have left Red Lion Square and gone to the new building. And –" she groped in her bag and produced an envelope, stamped with the words "Silver Dragon Film Company" – "that isn't all, though I doubt very much whether I should have accepted. My dancing does come first. I never meant to be an actress, let alone a film actress. Read it."

Rose read the letter slowly. It asked if Miss Drina Adams would be interested in having a film test with a view to taking the part of Ilonka in the film of *Diary of a Dancer*.

"Oh, Drina! You a film star! You *ought* to have the part – you were marvellous when you acted Ilonka in the play. But surely your grandparents won't take you away when you have this chance?"

"They know nothing about it," Drina said quickly. "And I shan't tell them. The letter was waiting for me when we got home yesterday and there were such a lot of others that I'm sure no one noticed it. I don't think I *would* have considered it, but – but it does make it harder somehow. I shall tell Miss Volonaise, but no one else."

"But Madam won't want you to go away. She'll tell your grandmother –"

"She and Mr Dominick evidently knew all about it before we went to Madeira. That's why I want to see her … just in case she should try to dissuade Granny even now. And – and to hear what she really thinks. I have to discuss it with someone, though it's silly of me really, because my mind's quite made up."

"They *shouldn't* ask it of you," Rose said fiercely. "You'd be quite all right with Miss Whiteway, or at that place where Joan and Sue live. You're almost sixteen, though no one would ever think it by the look of you. Everyone will say the same. Does Ilonka know?"

"Only you, so far. I haven't even written to Jenny, though she may telephone tonight. *She* gave up everything when her father went bankrupt. She'll never go to an agricultural college now. I can't moan to Jenny."

"Ilonka will have a fit," said Rose. Ilonka Lorencz was the third member of their trio. Ilonka and her family had escaped from Lynzonia a year or two before, and it was Ilonka's sister Terza who had written *Diary of a Dancer*, based on their experiences. "*Everyone* will have a fit. And I shall miss you … Oh, I just dread the winter now!"

"I'll miss you, too, but you'll have the others. I shall only have Antonia, who is nice, but doesn't really understand about my kind of life, and a lot of strange

girls. No boys, of course. I'm *used* to having boys around.
You must see the prospectus of the Selby Finishing
School. It just about made me sick when Granny showed
it to me last night. 'Girls are carefully chaperoned'. I
don't *need* chaperoning. I'm used to going my own way.''

Rose giggled, still rather shakily.

"Your granny has always over-protected you.''

"She's tried to, but I can look after myself. Good
gracious! I've been to Milan, New York and Paris. I've
met all sorts; I'm used to cities. And I'm going to be
chaperoned in Switzerland!'' Drina's voice was bitter,
though she tried to smile. "Anyway, don't let me moan. I
simply mustn't. I'm getting something that most girls
would give their ears for.''

Rose nodded gravely. She had only once been abroad,
when she and Drina went with the Dominick Company
to Paris during the previous spring. She longed to travel
and there was no doubt that Drina had been very lucky.
That she was still lucky, however, Rose did not believe.
Even a winter in the pleasant climate of the Ticino could
never, Rose saw clearly, make up for all that was being
left behind in London.

They talked for a while longer, then strolled on
through the gardens towards the Dominick Theatre,
which was on the Embankment, just before Waterloo
Bridge.

"We'd better go in through the front of the house,''
said Drina, as they approached the theatre. "Miss
Volonaise said to wait in the Circle and she'd come when
she could get away.''

"I wish we were coming on Monday,'' said Rose,
pausing to look at the new posters. The Dominick was
putting on a new ballet choreographed by Igor
Dominick, as well as *Les Patineurs* and a new production
of *Graduation Ball*.

'So do I. We were silly not to get seats. Not a hope now, of course." And Drina led the way confidently into the theatre. After a few words with the girl in the box office, whom they both knew, they climbed the broad stairs to the Dress Circle.

The company was at that moment dancing *Les Patineurs*. Drina and Rose stood for some minutes at the back watching the Blue Skaters, then sank quietly into seats near the centre aisle. The front of the Circle was fairly well filled, and amongst the audience Drina recognised the company ballet mistress, Igor Dominick himself, and Miss Adele Whiteway, her grown-up friend, who had designed the sets for the new Dominick ballet. But there was no sign of Marianne Volonaise.

Drina sat tensely, for once paying little attention to the ballet before her. She knew all the dancers by name and some were even almost friends. Bettina Moore, for instance, one of the Blue Skaters, had once been a lovely Little Clara, and Drina had later got to know her quite well in Italy. Then there was Judith Laurie, one of the youngest members of the *corps de ballet*, with whom she and Rose had sometimes gone about in Paris.

Drina jumped quite violently when a hand touched her shoulder lightly, and there was Marianne Volonaise, wearing a dark green dress that enhanced her dancer's figure.

"Come to the office, Drina. Rose will wait for you here."

Drina, with a fast-beating heart, rose and followed her. It still seemed strange that she could talk to Miss Volonaise as one human being to another, but she had wanted to speak to her even more than to Adele Whiteway, often the recipient of her confidences.

In the office the Director of the Dominick Company

and Ballet School indicated a chair and sat down herself.

"My dear girl! You look wholly Italian at this moment, not merely half! I suppose that's Madeira sunshine?"

"And on the ship going out, Miss Volonaise. We called at Gibraltar and Casabalanca, too. It was wonderful to see Morocco."

"But you look tired and strained. Do relax." Her gaze was on the clenched hand resting on the desk.

Drina flexed her fingers ruefully.

"I feel as stiff as anything. Miss Volonaise, I'm sorry if it was cheek – I believe Rose thinks it was – but I *had* to see you."

"My dear, I expected you. I nearly wrote and asked you to come here today. I really wished I could see you before you went away, but your grandmother was adamant. This is a most unfortunate business. I tried to talk her out of taking you with them, but I got nowhere. And, of course, you will get excellent ballet classes from Signora Lerrani. From the dancing point of view I'm not at all worried, but we hate to lose you. I had hoped that you would be able to persuade your grandmother to let you stay behind in London."

"I didn't try. I feel I *have* to go. Because of Grandfather, you see."

Marianne Volonaise sighed.

"Your grandmother was always obstinate. I don't believe that Mr Chester would let you go with them if he fully understood. He wants you, of course, but I don't think he'd ask such a sacrifice of you if he –"

"I really think I ought to go. I don't want him to know how I feel. I – I hate the thought of being away for so long. But – but that was why I wanted to see you, just in case you should say something to them. I've made up my mind and –"

Miss Volonaise glanced at the tense brown face and at

the shining black hair that fell so straight and thick almost to Drina's shoulders.

"*You're* obstinate, too. If you think it's right I won't say much more just now."

"I do think I must go."

"All right, then. But there's one thing, and I *was* going to put it to your grandparents. We're putting on *The Land of Christmas* in London this December and your old part of Jane is waiting for you. We need you, you know. We'll never find another Jane as good as you were last year in Francaster." She watched Drina intently, her face sympathetic and questioning.

Drina sprang to her feet.

"Oh, Miss Volonaise, I wish – I wish you hadn't told me!"

"I know. It seems mean, but you'd have heard before long, anyway. The news is getting about. Well, Drina?"

"I – I can't play Jane. It makes no difference. You know I can't."

The young girl and the elegant middle-aged woman eyed each other and then Marianne Volonaise's face softened.

"Very well. Do what you think's right. I admire you for it, though I don't think your grandparents should ever have planned to take you away. They left you when they went to Australia."

"Grandfather wasn't so – so frail then, and, in any case, they knew I was safe at Chalk Green. Grandfather *would* worry." Drina produced the letter from the film company. "There's this, too. But I wouldn't have done it."

"No," agreed Miss Volonaise, when she had read the letter, "I don't really think you would have had time for filming, though you might have enjoyed it. All right, Drina, go to Switzerland. Write to me sometimes and try to enjoy yourself. The change of climate will do you good, at least. No more damp winter air."

"I – I'd give anything for a London winter."

"You know you hate it, really." Marianne Volonaise took two tickets out of her bag. "Have you and Rose booked for Monday night?"

"No, Miss Volonaise. We've been wishing we had –"

"Then take these. Maybe it'll cheer you up."

"Oh, Miss Volonaise! Rose will be thrilled. Thank you very much."

"When are you going to Lugano? Shall we see you at the school before you leave? Term starts on the 10th."

"We're going to Milan that day, to see my Italian grandmother."

"Well, you'll like that. You're fond of her, I gather."

"Oh, yes. But it will be strange to see my grandmothers together."

Miss Volonaise nodded, completely understanding the remark. Drina's Italian father, who worked in London, had died when she was only a baby, and when Elizabeth Ivory had been killed in a plane accident a few months later the two grandmothers – Signora Adamo in Milan and Mrs Chester – had quarrelled bitterly over who should bring up the eighteen-month-old Drina. Mrs Chester had won and they had never seen each other since. But Drina's visit to Milan early the previous year had somehow smoothed things over at last and now the two women were ready to be reconciled.

"I do love Milan," Drina went on. "But – but just now I feel as though I'll never feel safe or enjoy anything again. Miss Whiteway says one never can feel safe, anyway, and that one must just get adjusted to the idea and enjoy life in spite of it."

"Adele Whiteway is a sensible and balanced woman," said Miss Volonaise. "You're lucky to have her for a friend. She'll always tell you the truth, as she sees it. She won't try to make things easy, but then there's never much value in that. You have to face life. By the way, did you know that our plans for building on the South Bank fell through?"

Drina jumped.

"The new Dominick School and rehearsal rooms, you mean? No, I didn't know."

"Various factors got in the way – money and difficulties over the land we had in mind. We've now negotiated for some land on the Euston Road near Warren Street Station. Building starts next week and we hope it'll be ready for the start of the summer term next year. It just *has* to be, as we're definitely out of Red Lion Square at the end of March. Term will end then, and the next one will start earlier than usual. Fortunately Easter will be early."

Drina sighed.

"Oh, it's all horrid! And that isn't a very nice part of London. I wish it could have been the South Bank if we just *have* to move."

"So do we, in some ways. But, after all, it isn't far from Regent's Park. You'll all be able to walk that way if you want exercise in the lunch-hour or after school. And there are plenty of trains and buses from all directions. Oh, well. I must get back to the rehearsal." She rose and put her hands for a moment on Drina's shoulders. "Cheer up, my dear. You're too intelligent not to get something from a change of scene. Remember Chalk Green and how you learned to love it."

"It was still the Dominick, really."

"Yes. Well, go back to Rose and stay as long as you want to. By the way, young Igor is quite desolated at the thought of your going."

"Igor doesn't really care whether I go or stay," Drina

said casually. Igor Dominick Junior was a year older than she was: a handsome, self-opinionated young man who was going to be a wonderful dancer, but who rather lacked some of the humanities.

"In his own way I think he does," said Igor's godmother, smiling.

She hurried away and Drina followed more slowly, hearing, as she approached the door at the back of the Dress Circle, the Strauss music of *Graduation Ball*.

2
Goodbye to London

At about the time when Drina and Rose were eating their lunch at a restaurant in the Strand Mr and Mrs Chester were just finishing their own meal. Mrs Chester fetched the coffee, poured it out and then settled herself more comfortably. She had been working hard all morning, compiling lists and doing a great deal of telephoning. For the flat in Westminster was to be given up in rather less than two weeks' time and the furniture was all to be stored until such time as they made other plans for living in London. Maybe, the following spring, they would take another flat away from the damp and mist of the river: St John's Wood or Primrose Hill, perhaps.

Meanwhile, there was also the packing to do for the winter in Switzerland, and they were taking linen and a good many other things to the villa.

"Drina *must* help me after this," she said, dropping two lumps of sugar into her coffee. "She's old enough to help and she's a good packer. I don't know why she had to stay out for lunch today of all days. Rose can't afford it, anyway."

"Remember that they'll be separated for some months," Mr Chester said rather reprovingly. He was devoted to his wife, but he often thought her very hard on Drina. Mrs Chester loved her grandchild deeply, but she was not always very sympathetic.

"Yes, I'm sorry about that, but Drina will have Antonia and that's a far more suitable friendship. Drina goes her own way, and Rose is a nice girl, with good manners, but her family isn't – well –"

"Don't let Drina hear you say so. She hates snobbishness, and so do I," he said, with a trace of sternness. "Rose may go as far as Drina. She has looks and personality and one gathers that she's a very good dancer."

"She didn't have Elizabeth Ivory for a mother," his wife remarked. "You know I never wanted Drina to be a dancer, but I can see that she's really got that something extra that makes a *great* dancer. Oh, I've no objection to Rose, but it won't hurt them to be separated for a few months. And it will undoubtedly benefit Drina to spend a winter away from London."

He sighed. As Drina had guessed, he was by no means convinced that they were doing the right thing, but he had been over-ridden by his wife's insistence, and his fears had been somewhat allayed by the cheerful way Drina had taken the news of her "exile" in the Ticino.

"She would have been perfectly all right with Adele Whiteway, or at that place where the Meredith twins live. I shouldn't have cared for it, in one way, and naturally I should have missed her. But –"

"Now, James, it's all settled, so don't start worrying about it all over again."

"I do worry. I wish I'd never agreed. But if Drina really isn't heart-broken ... she looks very tense sometimes. Anyway, we can try it for one term and then see –"

Mrs Chester didn't argue. She had won her point and

Drina was going with them to Switzerland. She was, in the first instance, thinking about her husband, but it was nevertheless a relief that she wouldn't have to worry about Drina left behind in London. Her granddaughter might be almost sixteen, but, in Mrs Chester's opinion, she was not always as sensible as she could be. Too much temperament and imagination.

"Inherited from her father," she thought, as she began to wash up. But it wasn't wholly true, and in her heart she knew it. Betsy Chester – later the great Elizabeth Ivory – had had her share of both imagination and temperament.

"I wish they'd both lived," Mrs Chester said to herself, not for the first time. "I don't know why life had to be so cruel as to take them both away when Drina was so young. It's meant that we had the pleasure of bringing her up, but it's been a responsibility, too, and by no means easy." She was conscious these days of feeling old, but maybe a winter by a beautiful lake would make all the difference.

After lunch Drina and Rose telephoned Ilonka, whose parents ran a restaurant, and Ilonka came to meet them as they walked along the Mall towards Green Park. Then, sitting on the grass under a tree in the park, the bad news had to be told all over again and Ilonka was horrified and upset.

"Oh, but, Drina, that is just wicked of your grandparents! We can't do without you, and – and you can't do without the Dominick. And the film and *The Land of Christmas* .. Oh, no, you can't go away to Switzerland!"

"They aren't wicked. Don't be silly, Ilonka," Drina said brusquely. "It's partly, at least, my choice. And I shouldn't have tried for the film. I do mind dreadfully

about the play, because I loved it last time. *And* about the Dominick –"

"At least you'll get away from Queenie and her dear cousin Sylvia," said Rose, who hated both rather unpleasant girls and was also rather afraid of them.

Drina and Ilonka groaned and then laughed.

"The so horrible Queenie!" said Ilonka, pulling a face.

"Sylvia is really horribler," Drina stretched herself out on the grass. "And she simply hates me. Now she'll always be top of the class. Oh, the Dominick hasn't always been peaceful lately, but I still hate leaving it."

"And Mark will mind, and Jan and Igor," said Ilonka.

"Mark has his own friends now. After all, he's in a higher class."

"But he was your friend from the Willerbury days."

The mention of Willerbury reminded Drina of Jenny, and the thought of her was at the back of her mind throughout that not very happy afternoon. Drina returned to the Westminster flat about four-thirty, in time for tea, and afterwards she and her grandmother settled down to making more lists. At six o'clock Drina went to her room and began to turn out the cupboards in an attempt to decide what winter clothes would be of use in Switzerland, but soon afterwards the telephone rang and it was Jenny.

"Oh, Drina, how are you? Did you have a wonderful time?" The familiar voice sounded cheerful enough, but it was the hard, bright cheerfulness that had been part of Jenny since her life changed, and it always sounded worse to Drina than if she had allowed herself to be miserable.

"Yes. Some of it was wonderful." The telephone was in the hall; the doors were all shut, but Drina dropped her voice. "Don't have too much of a shock. Grandfather has to spend the winter out of England and they've taken a villa near Lugano. I'm going, too, to the finishing school where Antonia goes."

There was a blank silence, then Jenny gasped:

"But the Dominick? Aren't you absolutely devastated? Oh, Drina, I *am* sorry!"

Drina mumbled into the telephone:

"Yes, I do mind, but I can't let them know. I'll write and tell you more about it. We're leaving on September 10th and staying in the Ticino until about April next year."

There was another short silence before Jenny said in a different voice,

"I think you're very brave. Didn't I tell you before you went to Madeira that there was something up?"

"You were right. As for brave ... How can *you* say that? Worse things happened to you and you bore them with – with stoicism."

"I bore them as best I could, and still am. But I know what it will cost you to be away from the Dominick, even if you *are* going to Switzerland. Meanwhile, I work!

"Oh, Jenny! Do you hate it?"

"The money's good," Jenny said coolly. "It's counted a good job. It *would* be for anyone who didn't yearn for the open air. But it's a five-day week, so I can still go farming at weekends. I've been to Brookes's as usual, and twice to Hogdens' on Sundays, though it's rather a long way. Robert and I got in part of the second hay crop single-handed last Sunday."

"I wonder where you'll be by the time I get home? Maybe you'll find a job you like better."

"I can't chop and change. I have to earn my living. I might be married, though."

Drina was silent with shock. Jenny had talked of marrying during their last meeting, but she had not taken it seriously.

"You – you couldn't be. To Robert, do you mean? You're too young ... Has he *asked* you?"

Jenny chuckled, sounding more like her old self.

"No, but he will one day. I shall be seventeen next June and I'm not a kid like you. I'm grown up. Oh, well, forget it. I can hear you gasping. I'll have to go. The phone bill. Why do you live so far away?"

Drina hung up and went slowly back to her room. Staring at the picture called *Manchester Valley* that she had bought at the Museum of Modern Art in New York, she struggled with the realisation that Jenny was, as she said, grown up. It did not really seem so very long, either, since she had been a plump child with thick fair hair. Little Jenny Pilgrim, who had hated ballet and always wanted to go farming.

Would she really marry red-haired Robert Hogden and become a farmer's wife? It would be the ideal solution, of course; the thing that Drina had often said in jest. But Jenny *married* ... Jenny with responsibilities ... children, perhaps.

Drina walked to the looking-glass and stared at herself. She *did* still look a child, as Jenny said. She wore a green cotton dress, childish sandals, and no make-up.

"But I'm not really a child," she told her reflected self, and she fell to dreaming of Grant Rossiter, whom she had met going to New York a year before, and again in Paris. She still loved Grant, warmly but rather sadly, for she could see no future for them at any time. Grant was four years older and one day he would meet and marry a pretty American girl, while *she* went on to be a dancer at the Dominick.

Then of course there was Igor – but who could ever take Igor seriously? And Jasper Blane, a dancer with the Lingeraux, who had seemed so much attracted to her in Madeira.

"Jenny doesn't know the half of it," Drina thought, and turned firmly again to her half-emptied cupboards. There was going to be little time for dreaming of any sort during the days to come.

They were certainly busy days and Drina did not try to get out of helping her grandmother. She packed and sorted and made endless lists, wrote labels and a dozen other things. There was some shopping to be done, too, for she needed new clothes for the winter. She had grown a little and some of her things were too short.

"But your Dominick suit and coat are really all right," Mrs Chester had said, frowning. "It's lucky that your new school has no uniform, and the Dominick clothes still fit. You must have a new coat for best, I suppose, and some dresses. You still have the white one that was bought in Paris."

"I shall need ski clothes, maybe." One of the things mentioned in the prospectus was that parties of girls were taken to Alpine resorts for winter sports.

"We can buy them in Switzerland, if you find you do need them. I don't know if you ought to do much skating or skiing. Think what a fuss you'd make if you injured yourself and couldn't dance."

Drina shuddered, entirely agreeing, though she longed to learn to ski.

But, though there was so much to do, Drina found time for her friends, and – since she was so soon to lose it – she found herself taking more than the usual pleasure in the London scene. Sometimes she caught her breath when she had unexpected glimpses: Buckingham Palace, with the Guards just moving away from the gates on a mellow early September morning ... the lights of Piccadilly Circus springing out at dusk ... the familiar red buses speeding over Waterloo Bridge ... the Houses of Parliament from the other side of the Thames.

Usually, when she knew she was going to a new
place, she learned all she could about it beforehand,
but, beyond buying a map of the Ticino, she did not do
so this time. She was trying to push all thoughts of
Switzerland away from her. All too soon she would be
an exile at a prim finishing school, with perhaps the
vineyards turning gold on the lower slopes of the
mountains and the lake blue in a hot autumn sun. There
might be compensations, but she was not looking for
them yet. She was living every possible moment of her
London life while she could.

With Ilonka she took a last look at the Dominick
School, even going into the entrance hall to look at her
mother's ballet shoes in their glass case. Ilonka did not
know that Elizabeth Ivory had been Drina's mother, but
she thought it perfectly natural that Drina should stand
there for a few minutes lost in thought. Ilonka loved the
Dominick, and, in company with every other student,
was fascinated and inspired by the life of the great
dancer.

Drina and Rose went to the Dominick Theatre to see
the new programme, and Drina thrilled to the Igor
Dominick ballet, which was very modern and danced to
Malcolm Arnold's music. They went to Covent Garden
on another occasion, sitting in the amphitheatre
because Rose never could afford more expensive seats,
and they saw *Symphonic Variations*, *Checkmate* and *The
Firebird*. *Checkmate* was a ballet after Drina's own heart;
she loved the Bliss music and sometimes dreamed of
one day dancing the Black Queen.

"Though I'm not likely to be tall enough," she said,
when they were stretching their legs in the interval.
"She needs to be so menacing."

"You're dark enough; you'd look wonderful."

They had both seen *The Firebird* a number of times, but

it never failed to cast its usual spell, and the wonderful music of the end part of the ballet, with the brilliant backcloth and the princes and princesses forming up for the final moments always made Drina's scalp prickle.

"I wonder *when* I shall be here again," she said sadly, as they descended the many stairs to Floral Street. "You must write and tell me about every single ballet you see, and all the news and everything. For I really shall be an exile this time."

Three days before the Chesters and Drina were due to leave London, Jasper Blane telephoned. The Lingeraux Company had returned from Madeira a few days before and had immediately started intensive rehearsals for the winter programme.

"But," said Jasper, in his pleasant and rather gentle voice, "I just *have* to see you, Drina, before you go away. Could you come out with me this evening?"

Drina hesitated, aware of his nervous breathing at the other end of the line. She knew that Jasper thought himself in love with her – maybe he *was* in love with her. In return she liked him, and was flattered by his obvious pleasure in her company, but there was still a lot to do and she knew very well that her grandmother would not be pleased if she accepted his invitation.

"I don't know, Jasper. I'm helping Granny. We're very busy. Where did you think of going?"

"I thought we could have a meal and then walk somewhere and – and talk. Oh, Drina, you'll be away for so long!"

He sounded so miserable that Drina gave in and went to ask her grandmother's permission. Mrs Chester had not really approved of Jasper, for she knew nothing of Drina's feelings for Grant and she thought her granddaughter still too young to go about with young men. She did not count Jan, Mark or even Igor Dominick; the first two were still young boys, in her estimation if not in their own, and Igor was the son of an old friend.

She heard the request with annoyance, but it was true that Drina would soon be far away from Jasper and she had certainly been very docile and hard-working during the past days.

"Oh, I suppose you may go, just this once. But you must be back early, mind."

So Jasper called for Drina at seven o'clock, looking very brown and fit after the time in the sun. He seemed nervous at first, but the pair set off cheerfully enough and were soon chatting very naturally, for Drina had to hear about the performances in Funchal that she had missed. Jasper took her to a small and obviously expensive restaurant in Soho and Drina was a little dismayed, knowing that he could not have all that much money, but she was too wise to protest and, after all, it was fun to be having dinner with a good-looking young man.

In fact, she felt very grown-up and sophisticated, and she thought wryly of the school where she would be so carefully chaperoned. It was an Italian restaurant and she was able to speak to the waiter in his own language, which seemed to impress Jasper.

"Just getting my hand in," she said modestly. "It will be all Italian, I suppose, in the Ticino."

Later, walking down Haymarket, they passed Queenie Rothington, who stared in undisguised interest at Jasper. She mumbled "Hullo!" and Drina said sweetly: "Hullo, Queenie", wondering if her old enemy knew yet that she would not be at the Dominick again for some time.

Drina and Jasper walked for some distance along the

Embankment towards Chelsea. It was a warm and golden evening, with sunlight glinting on the grey river. Jasper took her arm when they came to bridges, where the traffic surged past, and finally he took her hand and held it lightly but firmly.

"Oh, Drina, why are you going away? We might have met often during the winter. There's one thing, though. We're doing a short tour on the Continent in October and November. A week in Paris, a week in Munich and a few performances in Zurich and Basle. So I shall be in Switzerland, too, you see. I suppose you couldn't come up to Zurich? Or we might try and meet halfway. Would they let you?"

"I'm sure they wouldn't," Drina said regretfully. She found herself liking Jasper very much this evening, though she certainly wasn't at all in love with him. Besides, *any* familiar face would be welcome in Switzerland. "It's a long way from Lugano to Zurich, and, though they're supposed to take us on educational journeys, we're hardly likely to go to Zurich just when you're there."

"Will you write to me, then?"

"I might," she said cautiously. "But I shall have so many people to write to, and perhaps there won't be time. Do you know, there's an awful thing in the prospectus about the headmistress reserving the right to open girls' letters. Isn't that just too terrible? No one's ever opened my letters in my life, not even when I was little."

"Barbarous," agreed Jasper. "But maybe they're only protecting themselves in case of trouble. What kind of place is it?"

"I don't really know much about it, except the little bits Antonia has put into letters, and she doesn't often write. The girls are all quite old and they come from nearly every country in Europe. From outside Europe, too, probably. They'll be rich and pampered and they'll never have worked."

"Some people might say that you are rich and pampered," he said, remembering the expensive Funchal hotel where Drina had stayed with her grandparents, her pretty clothes and her general air of having everything. All this had saddened him as soon as he realised that he was attracted to her, for he only had the money he earned as a member of the Lingeraux *corps de ballet*.

"Oh, not in *that* way," Drina said impatiently. "We aren't well off now that Grandfather's retired. I think they're worried because the villa will cost such a lot."

"But this school must be costing a packet."

"I have my own money," she said and changed the subject. Jasper did not know much about her parents, beyond the fact that her father had been Italian.

Jasper saw her to the entrance of the block of flats, and they parted on the pavement under the interested gaze of the doorkeeper. He had known Drina for years and now she was old enough to have boyfriends. A very handsome young man, too!

Jasper would have liked to kiss Drina, but did not dare since she merely held out her hand.

"Goodbye. I shall think of you." And he walked abruptly away.

Then everything was ready, the cases and boxes were packed, and the last day came. It was only then that Drina wrote to Grant to tell him of her change of fortune: a brief, rather inhibited little note. She never allowed herself to reveal many of her deepest thoughts, though, in Paris, he had asked her to write to him sometimes.

Ilonka had planned a party for Drina's last evening in London, and her father had allowed her the use of a small room off the main restaurant, sometimes let for private gatherings. Rose went to The Golden Zither in the afternoon, to help with the preparations, but Drina – as guest of honour – was not invited until seven o'clock. So she spent a couple of hours with Adele Whiteway in the afternoon, drawing comfort from her friend's sympathetic manner. Adele would have been glad to take the girl for a few months, for her niece Lena, now a senior student at the Dominick, had gone back to live with her parents since they had come to London a few months before. But she had not tried to influence Drina in any way.

It turned out to be a wonderful party, for the Lorencz family employed a good chef. Mark, Igor, Jan Williams and three other boys from the Dominick were present, as well as the Meredith twins and Meryl, who were all in the same class. Drina's health was drunk with some specially concocted fruit cup – Igor was privately very scornful because there was no wine, but then he had grown up in Paris – and she replied rather shakily, for, now that the time for departure had almost come, she felt unbelievably miserable.

Afterwards the room was cleared and they danced and it was eleven o'clock before Drina went home in a taxi. London was lovely under a great full moon and the air that blew in through the open windows smelt faintly of autumn, though the trees were still green in the parks.

"London! Oh, London!" Drina murmured sadly.

Tomorrow everyone would return to the Dominick, and *she* would be on her way to Italy.

3

The School by the Lake

Though Drina did not get to bed until nearly midnight she had to be up early, because the flat was being cleared that morning. By lunch-time everything had gone except for the things that were going to Switzerland, and she took a last look round her bare little room, the room that she had had since before she was twelve. She had been miserable then, for she had not wanted to leave Willerbury, and she was miserable now. But there was no going back and she shrugged and went to join her grandparents. They were having a late lunch at a hotel near Victoria.

But by the time they were on the Channel ferry Drina had cheered up a little. She loved travel and at least, before she had to face the new school, she would see Milan again and her Italian grandmother.

She had rather hoped that they would travel to Milan on the Lötschberg line, so that she would have a glimpse of Kandersteg and also experience again that wonderful rush along the precipice above the Rhone Valley. But, as Mr Chester was intending to spend one night in Lugano, to see that all was ready at the villa, their reservations had been made by way of the Gotthard line.

It was a lovely evening and the Channel was calm and blue. Drina stood on deck most of the time, watching the approaching coastline of France. It seemed a long time since she had journeyed to Paris with Rose and Adele Whiteway and her heart lifted as they edged towards the quay at Calais and she saw the porters waiting volubly for the gangways to be put across.

Mrs Chester had done plenty of travelling in her time, in the days when her daughter Betsy was dancing in many capitals, but Drina was amused and a little flattered and touched to find that now *she* was regarded as the experienced traveller. It was almost the first time that her grandmother had treated her as a really sensible person, and this was at least partly because her French was good; quite good enough to be well understood by their elderly and rather sardonic-looking porter.

It was already dusk as they walked along the high, seemingly endless train to the sleeping-cars and she was sharply conscious of being in another country. It was the smells mainly ... garlic and cigar smoke and the very smell of the train.

The Chesters were sharing a two-berth compartment, and Drina was rather dismayed to find that there was another berth in hers. But the attendant shrugged and smiled and told her, in French, that she would probably have it to herself. And this proved to be the case.

Drina stood in the corridor as the train jogged away from Calais and Mrs Chester looked out to say:

"We get to Basle early, so why don't you go to bed?"

"I will soon, Granny. I'm just savouring being in France. I do love the feel and smell of it."

Mrs Chester received the remark in silence, for she always thought Drina too intense in her reactions. But she was glad, when at last she was in her narrow and rather stuffy berth, that at least her granddaugher was apparently getting some pleasure from the journey. In her heart she still felt guilty because she had been so firm in her resolve to take Drina with them.

Drina chose the top berth as being more airy. She was soon in bed, but she did not sleep for a long time. The train was now rushing along at a great speed, roaring and swaying, and her mind was filled with pictures of the last days in London and haunted by doubts of the future.

Rose, Ilonka, Igor, Miss Whiteway ... she would not see any of them for more than six months. Rose and Ilonka would idle their way home from the Dominick School without her on fine afternoons, probably wandering through the narrow streets near the Opera House and parting in Piccadilly Circus. The thought was a sharply painful one. She was not jealous by nature, but the other two would have each other and their friendship, until now probably held together mainly by her own presence, would grow. They would be older and maybe different when she returned to London at last. *She* would be older and different, too. For there was no stopping growth and the passing of the days and weeks.

In a way the last thought was a comfort, for the time *would* pass. Some day she would go back, though not to Westminster and not to Red Lion Square. She would be able to look back at this Drina Adams who was being carried so rapidly across Europe. Maybe a day would come when she would go to one of the farms with Jenny, and they would sit on a wall and talk. Or would Jenny really be married? Not before she was seventeen, surely? Her parents would never agree to that – the very thought was still fantastic.

And then Drina remembered Grant. In London she was far from him; in Switzerland she would be further away still. Not that a few hundred extra miles could really make much difference.

Wooing sleep, she began, in imagination, to walk down Fifth Avenue from the Plaza, seeing it all clearly in the hot autumn sunshine. The spires of St Patrick's Cathedral … the tapering finger of the RCA Building … the high tower of the Empire State Building still ahead. She had reached the New York Public Library at 42nd Street when she fell asleep.

Breakfast on the station at Basle; red and white table-clothes, black cherry jam, and the smell of good coffee. Mrs Chester, who had not slept well, was tired and rather irritable, but she cheered up when they and their luggage were safely on the second train.

Drina sat in a dream, watching the neat, bright landscape flying past. Chalet-type houses, with shutters and window-boxes, fields where the corn had been cut, wooded hills, even factories. It was not the Switzerland of popular imagination, but she had seen it before and knew that more dramatic scenes would come. And when, at last, they were speeding along the shores of Lake Lucerne she went to stand in the corridor, all misery forgotten in sheer pleasure in the blue lake water and higher mountains. When they stopped at stations and she leaned out, the sun was hot and the light had a sharp, hard glitter that brought out colour and outline.

Things grew more and more wonderful as they began to speed towards the real mountains, the snow-capped Alps that lay to the south. The snowfields were shining with an unreal brilliance and just before they stopped at Göschenen Drina saw a view up a long valley that made her cry out. Such a vast glacier and snowfield, seeming to hang in the air!

"Oh, I'd *forgotten* what it felt like to see the Alps! I'd quite forgotten. If only I could get out and walk!"

Mrs Chester frowned, for she thought that people would think Drina peculiar in her enthusiasm. But Mr Chester laughed.

"Maybe we'll spend Christmas in Andermatt or Kandersteg: one of the high places. It does look wonderful." There was colour in his own cheeks, for the glorious views had made him feel more alive than for a long time. Even the flowers and the bare rocky peaks of Madeira had not been so uplifting to the spirit.

But almost at once they were roaring through the great Gotthard tunnel, on and on through the noisy darkness, and when they emerged again at Airolo it was, seemingly, into a different land. There were still high mountains, and, looking back, Drina could still see snow on the southern slopes of the Gotthard Alps, but this scene was rockier and more sun-drenched. Or somehow drenched in a different sun – hotter and more like Italy.

Down and down and down, close to a tumbling river, until there were cypresses and vineyards and faded pink and cream buildings that seemed wholly Italian. The baked fields were sometimes bordered with the strange granite slabs of the Ticino and the little coloured churches, some of them high on the mountains, had tiny open belfries.

It was hard to believe that this was still Switzerland and something deep in Drina's being responded to the heat and the little stone villages, to the sun-tanned, dark-haired people working in the fields, some of the men in faded blue trousers, naked to the waist. For a little while, at least, it no longer seemed such a hardship that she was to live in the Ticino for months.

Bellinzona had three castles on its vine-clad hills; then the valley began to open out. Mrs Chester started to gather together her husband's things.

"Drina, the moment we reach Lugano you are to get a porter for your grandfather. I don't suppose we stop long and all the boxes have to be taken out of the luggage van. Can you manage that?"

"Oh, sure, Granny," Drina said confidently.

"Let us have no Americanisms. You know I don't like them. Of course the porter *may* speak English. James, are you sure you'll be all right? I wish now –"

"Of course, my dear. I'll arrange for the stuff to be sent up to the villa and you know that the estate agent is to meet me there. He writes excellent English, and I presume he speaks it. I'll do nothing to exhaust myself. I'll have an early dinner at the hotel and get a good night's sleep. Drina can meet me at the Stazione Centrale at twelve tomorrow."

"Not alone," said Mrs Chester, rather distractedly straightening his jacket.

"Bless me, yes. Didn't she meet the Dominick Company nearly eighteen months ago? Give my regards to Andrina and tell her I'm looking forward to meeting her."

Then there was Lake Lugano, bluer than anything they had seen, with coloured villas climbing up the slopes of Monte Bré, and Monte San Salvatore, with its wooded slopes, at the western end of the town. The station was high above the lake and the platform was dazzling in the sun. Drina leaned out, catching the eye of a young and alert-looking porter. He came running to her side as the train stopped.

"You want a porter? You have luggage?" he asked in

Italian. It was perhaps the measure of her un-English appearance that he seemed not at all surprised when she answered in the same language.

The last they saw of Mr Chester he was standing on the platform with a small mountain of trunks and boxes around him. The train sped away round the lake, with Drina still leaning out of the window.

"Do come in, child. You'll lose your head if we go through a tunnel."

"Granny, where is the villa and where the school?"

Mrs Chester gestured vaguely towards Monte Bré.

"The villa is towards Cassarate, I think, and the school is this side, more or less in Paradiso. I doubt if I should enjoy this place in summer – far too many tourists – but in autumn and winter no doubt it will be heaven."

Mrs Chester sank down again and closed her eyes. They now had the first-class compartment to themselves, but Drina was too restless to settle, as the train sped over the bridge that spanned the lake. Everywhere looked colourful and unbelievably lovely … the higher mountains could still make her heart beat faster, though here there was almost no snow even on the highest peaks. It had been a hot, dry, summer.

But – oh, if only it were just a holiday! They had had lunch some time before and now it was nearly two o'clock. In London, at the Dominick, classes would be starting again. Rose and Ilonka had planned to sit together … It was just no use thinking about it. It was not, after all, as bad as that terrible departure from Willerbury so long ago. Then Drina had been forbidden ballet; now her practice clothes and all her shoes were in the trunk that had gone to the villa. Her precious mascot Hansl she had with her in the suitcase on the rack. Hansl had seen many different places; he had even stood on dressing-tables in theatres in Genoa and New York. But he had never adorned the bedroom of a finishing-school. It seemed rather absurd to think of the little cat in such a place.

There were few formalities at the frontier town of Chiasso and then they really were in Italy, going on towards Como and then across the plain to Milan. Excitement welled up in Drina as the city drew near. She had loved it and felt at home there, and it would be good to see her Italian grandmother again.

Signora Adamo was standing by the barrier, an extremely stylish, pretty woman, who looked nothing like her age. She looked, in fact, very many years younger than Mrs Chester. Though she had known sorrow, her life had for many years been leisurely and on the whole happy and the fact showed.

The two women eyed each other and it was Signora Adamo who came forward to shake hands with Mrs Chester and to kiss Drina warmly on both cheeks.

"It is so pleasant to see you," she said in excellent English to Mrs Chester, and Drina thought how strange it was that these two who had once fought so bitterly should now be meeting under happier circumstances.

"And to see you," Mrs Chester said, a little stiffly, but it was just her manner. She never found it easy to unbend.

"And you had a pleasant journey? James is well? Drina, I can see, is very well. She has grown and she is so pretty –"

"The journey was tiring," Mrs Chester said hastily. She did not think it good for Drina to be complimented. "James is quite well, thank you. He'll be arriving tomorrow morning."

"We will get a taxi at once. You'll both want to go to your hotel. I was so sorry not to have room at my flat for all of you. But the building where I live has an excellent restaurant. I hope you'll both have dinner with me this evening."

The porter and the two adults walked away down the vast hall of the Stazione Centrale and Drina followed slowly, hearing Italian on every hand, remembering that other arrival when she had been shy and strange and rather scared. Now it all seemed familiar, but none the less exciting for that.

They drove away from the grand pillars of the station, round some gardens and into the heart of the busy city. In the hot afternoon the sun struck the pavements dazzlingly and people sauntered along in the thinnest of summer clothes. Summer was almost over, but no one would have thought so.

Drina, listening to the conversation between her two grandmothers, gazed out at the city to which she half belonged, and where – but for fate, in the shape of Mrs Chester's determination – she might have spent her life. It was very satisfying to be back in Italy.

The days in Milan flew by all too rapidly. After an initial tussle with Mrs Chester, Drina went about mostly on her own. She did not mind the heat, in fact, she blossomed in it, and she was an excellent walker. She went to the Cathedral again, wandered in the Piazza del Duomo, re-acquainted herself with the Galleria Vittorio Emanuele, and went over to Santa Maria delle Grazie to look again at the Last Supper in the adjoining refectory.

The Piazza del Duomo, in particular, was haunted by memories of her last visit. There she had been furious with Igor because – not knowing her then – he had taken her for a child. There she had made friends with Bettina Moore, and, over by the shop at the entrance to the Galleria, she had talked to Miss Volonaise.

There was no ballet on at La Scala, but there was opera, and Signora Adamo had taken seats for *La Traviata*. So Drina entered the famous opera house again, wearing the white Paris dress and a beautiful new necklace that had been a present from her Italian grandmother. She did not know much about opera, nor greatly care for it, but it was a thrill to be there and goodness only knew when she would enter any kind of theatre again.

She made the most of the evening, being moved more than she had expected by the glorious singing. For some time it had been said that a Dominick Opera Company was to be started, but for various reasons this had not happened yet. In Milan, that night, was born a faint feeling for opera that Drina intended some day to develop. It was silly not to try to understand and appreciate this great branch of the theatre.

Wherever she went she was taken for Italian, until she had to speak at length. Her Italian accent was good, but she was out of practice and her vocabulary was not large. It would no doubt be improved at the Lugano school, where languages were of the utmost importance, but she supposed sadly that she would have few opportunities of exercising her knowledge in the town itself. The last days of freedom were precious, for she genuinely felt as though she were going to a kind of prison. The very thought was so depressing that she always pushed it away.

Mr and Mrs Chester spent most of the time at the flat with Signora Adamo, though they did go for one or two drives in the cool of the evening.

"Drina is so adult, so well able to take care of herself," said Signora Adamo, when Drina returned one afternoon to find them all drinking tea and eating delicious little cakes.

"I wouldn't call her very adult yet," said Mrs Chester, eyeing Drina's flushed cheeks. "And I do not approve of the calm way she walks about alone. Now James is different. He abets her."

"You can't try to keep her a child for ever."

"I don't try, but she won't be sixteen for a few weeks yet. I thought the Italians chaperoned their daughters."

"So they do, but Drina is an international. One feels she can look after herself."

"And so I can," said Drina, accepting tea.

"The Gardinos were on the telephone while you were out," said Mr Chester. "They seem a little cross because we aren't visiting Genoa this time. We're to meet Antonia at the station here about eleven o'clock tomorrow. As you know, she's spending one night at the villa."

"Both girls will have to help to get the boxes unpacked," said Mrs Chester. "It will be nice to see Antonia again. I liked her so much when she visited us. But she must realise that we can't treat her as a guest when there'll be so much to do."

Both Drina and her grandfather laughed.

Antonia looked just as pretty as Drina remembered, and it was a relief to realise how much she liked her cousin, when they would be close companions for so long. But Antonia, for all her charm and warm interest in her cousin's affairs, did not, as Drina had once said, understand about the dedicated life of a dancer. She admired Drina for being a ballet dancer, and was even inclined to be very much overawed by the professional appearances her cousin had made both in ballet and straight plays, but she had no knowledge of what it meant in terms of hard work and even near heartbreak.

They drove to the villa – called the Villa Mimosa –

through the hot afternoon light, and it turned out to be, as Mr Chester had reported, a very delightful place, standing in a large garden not far from the lake, with green shutters and walls half-covered with wisteria that would be fountains of purple in the spring. It was not a large house and would be easy enough to manage, with the help of a young Italian-Swiss girl who came in every day. Lucia would shop and cook, as well as help with the housework, and she seemed a cheerful girl and very willing, the eldest of a large family and already quite skilled in the running of a house.

Antonia borrowed an overall from Lucia and set to work to help with the unpacking and sorting, because she, too, was quite well trained, and as they worked she chattered in a mixture of English and Italian, telling Drina about the Selby Finishing School.

"Oh, it is quite a pleasant place. Very English, of course. See how my English has improved! But of course we must speak Italian for you. Miss Selby was once a teacher at a school in the Oberland, but she wished to start her own and that is two – perhaps three – years ago. She is very nice. ...Oh, middle-aged, I suppose, and very eager that all shall be *comme il faut*. The French have the best words for that! We must behave well ... we must not make eyes at young men, nor giggle in the streets. She regards the young men as – as ogres," said Antonia, coming out with the English word after hesitation. "Some of the English and American girls think she is silly to make so much of the fuss about young men. At home they go out with whom they please. But Miss Selby is anxious ... the good name of her school one supposes, of course, and then two terms ago there was trouble. A girl eloped. Yes, *eloped*, with a handsome young man from Fribourg. He was on holiday and then, it seems, they corresponded and it was a great passion."

"Good heavens!" cried Drina, fascinated and amused by all this. Appalled, too, because soon the rules would apply to *her*. "What happened?"

"Oh, she was caught very quickly and then her parents were asked to take her away. They sent her to Paris, to live with a strict lady who would see that she did not elope again. She was only seventeen. It was very shocking," said Antonia solemnly, but with dancing eyes.

Drina's room, that she was to occupy at weekends, had a tiny balcony and there was a view of the lake through chestnuts and tall cypresses. She was, of course, taking most of her possessions to school, including one or two of her pictures. She had chosen to take two of the little prints that Grant had bought her in Paris, for there was no hope that there would be room for her big one of Manchester Valley. This she had packed unframed, and her grandfather promised to have it reframed and have it ready for her first visit to the villa. It was oddly comforting to think that it would be there when she came home for weekends.

There was an extra bed in Drina's room and this Antonia was to have. She continued her chattering when they were sent to bed early, lying in the dark, seeing the distant glitter of lights on the hills across the lake and the high gleam of the stars.

"Last term I shared a bedroom with a French girl and one who is English. But Miss Selby wrote to my parents to say that this term I would be with you and Tamina Rionante."

So there was no hope of a room to herself and Drina did not much like sharing for any length of time. She had only rarely shared at all, apart from the ten months at Chalk Green. There would be no place where she could retreat and hide; no complete quiet for dreaming.

"Tamina," Antonia was continuing, "is, I think, quite nice. I do not know her well. She is Swiss, from the Ticino – she lives near Locarno, I believe – but to you she will seem very Italian. She is one who learns ballet."

This was better, but Antonia was still going on:

"I think she is quite a beginner, though I heard that she used to learn when she was younger. She was at Miss Selby's other school in the Oberland, where there was, one gathers, no ballet. She is very pretty, this Tamina. You'll like her, I think. She is one of the youngest."

Well, even someone who was quite a beginner at ballet might be better than no one.

They had breakfast on the terrace, in the shade of mimosas and oleanders. It was beautiful there and Drina would have given almost anything for life to go on as it was for a long time. But they were to be at the school in time for lunch. She and Antonia snatched a couple of hours in which to explore the ancient arcades and narrow, cobble-stoned streets of the old part of Lugano, and then that was the end, as Drina thought in despair, of freedom.

At twelve o'clock they were back at the villa and soon afterwards the taxi arrived. Then, with all the luggage, Mrs Chester and the two girls were driven through the town and round the far side of the lake, until Monte San Salvatore reared up above them.

The taxi turned in through some wide open wrought-iron gates and drove up a long, tree-shaded avenue to where a large white house stood surrounded by glowing gardens. This house, too, had shutters and balconies, but the paint was bright blue. Over the sun-baked lawns a few young girls were walking and these stopped talking to stare at the new arrivals.

Antonia waved and was recognised, and then all eyes were on Drina, so small in the low heels that Mrs Chester preferred her to wear.

"They think," said Antonia, who was five feet eight and wore high heels, anyway, "that I have brought my little sister. You will be the baby ... the youngest."

Drina did indeed feel very young as she and her grandmother walked through the cool entrance hall. Suddenly it was all totally improbable ... a nightmare from which she had to wake. If it were real it felt rather like entering a convent. The Dominick had never seemed further away.

4

An Exile Indeed

Miss Selby was sitting at a desk in a pretty room that had long windows wide open to a small, enclosed garden: probably her own private domain. She was about forty, smartly dressed, but with a plain, sensible face.

Mrs Chester was immediately reassured, for this was the type of woman of whom she instinctively approved. Drina, on the other hand, sank into even deeper dismay, if that were possible. She had an instant, heart-stabbing picture of Miss Volonaise, with her dancer's figure and her Paris clothes. Even Miss Lane, headmistress of the Dominick Ballet School, had not this air of commanding common sense to the exclusion of everything else. Miss Lane dealt with propective dancers and was a woman of imagination. Drina, quick and often surprisingly accurate at sizing up character, knew at once that there was little imagination here, though there might be plenty of ordinary kindness.

Miss Selby, in her turn, liked Mrs Chester almost before they had exchanged a dozen words, and she received the small, dark new girl with relief. The girl looked so young and demure in her crisp dress and certainly not the type of girl she had rather apprehensively expected. For Miss Selby heartily disapproved of "theatre children" and she could get plenty of rich and important pupils without accepting anyone who seemed unsuitable. But she liked Antonia and had felt it difficult in this case to refuse a recommendation from Signora Gardino.

She liked her girls to learn ballet, for she thought it gave confidence and good deportment and it was useful for end-of-term performances. But this Drina Adams (Adamo, really, but it had been stressed that the girl was always known by the English version of her name) was to have an hour free for practising every morning without fail, and there had been letters from Mr Dominick and Miss Volonaise stating that, for her, ballet was as important as ordinary classes.

Miss Selby was the daughter of a Cambridge don and had herself taken an excellent degree at that University. Languages were her subject and she had travelled a good deal. She had acquired some measure of sophistication during the years and felt herself more than able to deal with the girls of many nationalities who came to her for a year, or sometimes longer. But she did not in the least admire ballet as an art, and had, in fact, little feeling for the theatre.

Drina sat tensely, swallowing with difficulty, as Miss Selby and her grandmother talked. It was years since she had felt so miserable and helpless, so utterly alien. She jumped when Miss Selby addressed her again.

"I believe you're quite a clever girl? I gather you speak Italian and French fairly fluently. How about German?"

"A – a little, Miss Selby. I have a German friend and – and I thought I was going to Germany this summer. I could learn more quite quickly."

"Good! We speak French at breakfast one morning and German the next. Then usually Italian at lunch-time and English during the evening meal. You'll find us very international."

"Yes. I – I see."

"What a mouse," thought Miss Selby, and then, catching a flash of the very dark eyes, was not so sure. Girls who had been at a co-educational school, and who had also been professional dancers and actresses since they were thirteen could never be "mice", surely?

"You'll be sharing a room with your cousin and Tamina Rionante. But unfortunately Tamina has measles and won't be returning for a while yet. Perhaps you would both like to see over the house?"

"Very much," said Mrs Chester, who was privately appalled by Drina's face. Good heavens! She looked as though – as though – Mrs Chester could find no words for the look of withdrawn despair.

They set off on a tour of the house, which was delightful in every way. Flowers everywhere, shining floors, space, sunlight and modern equipment. The bedrooms were large and airy, divided by attractive curtains, the classrooms held folding desks and plenty of flowers and new books, as well as prints on the walls. There was a library, two huge sitting-rooms for the girls, with comfortable chairs and a record-player and television in each. The dining-room, where the polished tables were laid for lunch, would not have disgraced an expensive hotel.

Mrs Chester commented favourably on everything, but Drina showed no real interest until they crossed the garden to a new building that turned out to contain an art room and a very large, beautiful studio. Gazing at the mirrors and the *barre* Drina felt a little better.

Miss Selby saw her change of expression and said kindly:

"This is where you will practise from nine o'clock

until ten every morning. That's what you want, isn't it?
You are to have the studio entirely to yourself. Signora
Lerrani comes on Wednesday and Friday afternoons.
The other girls who learn ballet are supposed to
practise, but I'm afraid they're rather remiss about it
and then Signora Lerrani isn't pleased."

"*I* shall practise," said Drina, and could not keep the
touch of arrogance out of her voice.

"It wouldn't occur to her to miss," said Mrs Chester,
who was feeling much unwilling sympathy for her
grandchild. She recognised that it would take courage
and determination to keep on alone and once more the
feeling of guilt assailed her.

A gong sounded in the house behind them and Miss
Selby said:

"Lunch in five minutes. Of course many of the girls
won't arrive until afternoon or early evening."

"I must go," said Mrs Chester, glancing at her watch.

"Well, I hope that Drina will be very happy with us.
As it is Wednesday now I suggest that she remains with
us this weekend. Then a week on Friday, after school,
she shall be sent over to you in a taxi."

"I can walk," said Drina, almost with a croak. "Or
take the bus."

Miss Selby still smiled very kindly.

"I am not sure if I should be able to spare a member of
the staff to accompany you. A taxi will be best. It's quite
a long way, after all."

"She's used to going about by herself everywhere,"
said Mrs Chester, rather faintly. Even she could see
that, from Drina's point of view, this was monstrous.

"Of course what she does when she is in your care is
nothing to do with the school. But we prefer that girls
shall not leave the school unaccompanied. It must seem
rather silly," said Miss Selby, suddenly much more

human. "But there are good reasons, and most of the parents – especially the French and Italian ones – prefer it."

She tactfully left Mrs Chester and Drina to say goodbye in the hall and then Mrs Chester went rather hurriedly out to the taxi that had been waiting all the time.

Drina, struggling with a variety of emotions, was almost at once pounced on by Antonia, who looked flushed and animated.

"Miss Selby says to take you in to lunch and you can unpack afterwards. What did you think of her?"

"I – I don't know." Drina could not have said more if her life had depended on it.

"The girls are most eager to meet you. They cannot believe that you'll soon be sixteen."

Drina couldn't believe it, either. The girl who had dined with Jasper Blane seemed a world away. She only wanted to be alone to cry. But she was proud and was not going to admit this even to Antonia.

The tables were only about a third filled and the girls already present seemed to be mostly Italian and Swiss. They were an attractive lot, well dressed and all, except for a German girl called Lotti, who sat on Drina's right, wore make-up. Some looked quite grown up and Antonia whispered that the lovely Italian girl, Francesca, would soon be nineteen.

"She is to marry in the spring – a wonderful match. She is here because she will need to speak many languages. Her fiancé is a diplomat."

Lotti reminded Drina of her German friend Hildegarde. Lotti came from Augsburg and knew Dinkelsbühl, where Hildegarde now lived.

"I was to visit her in August, but I went to Madeira instead," said Drina, making little headway with the tasty soup followed by veal, French fried potatoes and salad.

"You travel much?" asked Lotti politely.

"Oh, yes. Quite a bit. And I shall travel even more when – if I get into the Dominick Ballet Company."

The other four girls at the table were passionately interested in the new arrival, for Antonia had stressed her importance. Most of them, unlike Miss Selby, loved the theatre and were not wholly ignorant of what it might mean to be both a dancer and an actress. But they saw that she was almost unable to talk, let alone eat, and presently they chatted about their own affairs in a mixture of languages, for it did not matter which they spoke on the first day.

Antonia continued to murmur information occasionally.

"Bianca comes from Milan; she is one who learns ballet. Gertrud is from Zurich; her father is a banker. Lotti is a dull girl – oh, she can't hear, she is too interested in the pudding."

"But she looks nice."

"Ah, but dull!" repeated Antonia, with a twinkle. "The only one with no boyfriend. All, all of us have boyfriends at home, and Francesca is not the only one who is engaged. Tell me, Drina, it is a long time since we met. Have you a boyfriend?"

The question was heard and all conversation stopped. Bianca giggled.

"She is too young. She's not American. Now we know that American girls – think of Ethel Benkoff. *She* says she had her first date when she was twelve."

"I know plenty of boys," said Drina coolly. She had to live with these girls and she was not going to be stamped as the "baby", even if she was the youngest in age.

"But plenty? How is that? Does your grandmother then permit that you –?"

"I go – went – to a co-educational school."

"With *boys*? In the school with you, like America? But Antonia says it is a dancing school."

"Well, boys learn to dance, too. We mostly have ballet classes separately until we're older but we do all ordinary lessons together. Co-education is quite usual in Britain."

"That must be – very funny."

"It's quite natural. I've worked with them since I was twelve."

"But the special boy?"

"Oh, he –" said Drina, adopting Jasper, since she could not bring herself to mention Grant – "is quite old. He's a dancer with another company."

This caused quite a sensation, and there was so much noise at their table that one of the members of staff, who was sitting at the next table, turned round.

"Quiet, girls. Do you shriek like that at home, Bianca?"

"But no, Miss Green. Never," said Bianca meekly.

"Then please don't do it here."

"Miss Green teaches us music," Antonia whispered. "She is very nice, really. Not usually cross. And over at Francesca's table is Madame Maréchel, who takes French literature. All of the staff are not here yet, or else they lunch with Miss Selby."

The meal was over at last and Antonia led Drina to the room they were to share with Tamina. The curtains were all drawn back and there were two big windows, both with a view of the lake through the trees. The third cubicle would be windowless and Drina looked at it sadly, for the view of blue water and high bare mountains was lovely.

"You may have a window this term," said Antonia

generously. "The other we must leave for Tamina, I think. She wouldn't mind, perhaps, but it is fair, for she has been here longer than I myself."

"But, Antonia, don't you *mind*?"

Antonia shook her head and just then the school matron arrived, an attractive French-Swiss, wearing a white nylon overall and carrying a bunch of keys.

"You are Drina Adams? How do you do? Antonia, you'll help her to unpack? Girls are arriving every minute – there was a train from the North just now. If I can help you –"

"Matron! Matron!" shrilled a voice from the corridor. "Would you believe it? I don't have my blue case ... I guess I must have left it in the taxi –"

"Ethel Benkoff!" groaned Matron and hurried away.

"It's really terribly nice of you, Antonia," said Drina starting to drag her trunk into one of the window cubicles. "Anyway, you can share my view whenever you want to."

"But no," said Antonia. "After today the curtains must always be kept closed when we are in here."

"Oh, for heaven's sake! Why?" It would ensure some privacy, but to make a rule of it –

Antonia shrugged.

"I don't know. It is just so. There are many rules."

"Far too many. I shall stifle. Over the rules, I mean, not through lack of air." And Drina took her keys out of her bag and began to unpack fiercely, flinging clothes in all directions. Antonia, abandoning her own unpacking, began to whisk them into the right places.

"Dresses in the cupboard in the corridor, see. Shoes on the floor of the cupboard. All the small things in the bureau. Coats and things like winter boots – but you will not need them for a long time, unless it turns very wet – downstairs."

"I suppose I can put up my pictures? Or is there a rule about *that*? I've brought those little hooks that go into the wall."

"Pictures are permitted. There'll just be room each side of the window. Oh, Paris! How pretty!"

There were also small framed pictures of groups at the Dominick and these Drina put on her bureau, with Hansl. By the time she had finished she felt utterly wretched again and the day, let alone the term, stretched endlessly ahead. There seemed few rules on the first afternoon and new arrivals were constantly looking into the room. The American, Ethel, came to meet Drina and to explain that her case had not been lost after all.

"It was in another room. Bianca found it just as Matron was going to call the taxi place."

"Ethel comes from Trenton, New Jersey," said Antonia. "Drina has been to New York. She is in love with it; she wishes always to go back."

"My brother's at Columbia, but I haven't seen the States for two years," Ethel said cheerfully. She had a snub nose and fair hair. "My father is working in Paris. Heavens! I didn't want to come back to the nunnery, but I must say it's great to see everyone. Have you seen Flora's ring? Let me tell you something. I think I'll get engaged myself and surprise you all."

By teatime – Miss Selby liked to abide by English institutions – the whole building was buzzing with talk, and by then Drina had a headache and only wanted to escape. But where, in this place, could she hope to be alone?

At first even the attempt was impossible, because the English teacher, Miss Marlow, captured her to discuss her time-table.

"You're to take exams when you go back to England,

I understand? I've a list of your subjects, and of course
we also give a lot of time to art, music and languages.
You're taking French as a subject, of course. Nine
o'clock to ten – yes, your ballet practice. Well, we'll try
this for a week or two and see how you go on. Things
are quite elastic here. Much of the work is done in study
groups and not in large classes. Some of the older girls
give most of their time to special subjects. You look very
young. Only fifteen, aren't you?"

"S – sixteen at the end of next month."

Miss Marlow patted her shoulder reassuringly.

"Cheer up. It must be a great change for you, but
you'll like it here. The girls are a high-spirited crowd –
too high-spirited sometimes." She laughed. "And you'll
have your cousin."

But Antonia amongst her friends was no real help.
There was no doubt that most of the girls looked nice,
and the fact that they were of so many nationalities was
not the thing that made them so totally alien.

"Perhaps I'm narrow-minded," Drina thought
wretchedly, hesitating in the hall. "I've given most of
my time to ballet for so long. And everyone but Jenny is
connected with it. Even Jenny has *some* idea. Do this lot
think of *nothing* but clothes and boys? I'm – I'm as alien
as if I came from the moon. I wonder what Rose would
think?"

But it was dangerous to let her thoughts dwell on her
friend, and she made hastily for a side passage as a new
taxi-load arrived at the front door.

The passage led her to another door that gave on to
the garden, on the side away from the lawns and
flower-beds. There were trees and bushes near and
Drina dived towards them, arriving with a gasp in the
hot green shade. Some of them were tall semi-tropical
shrubs and insects buzzed under the leaves. But she

pushed her way unheedingly until she came to a tiny clearing, where she flung herself down and burst into tears. They were the first tears she had shed since that awful afternoon high above Funchal and once she had started to cry she couldn't stop. It was the long overdue explosion of tension and a great relief.

She cried for a long time, only half-aware of voices and laughter in the distance. But at last the tears stopped and she lay on the warm earth, feeling weak and almost ready for sleep. But she certainly could not sleep, when someone might be noticing her absence. She still had her bag with her and she gasped with horror when she saw her face in her tiny looking-glass. It was dirty and swollen.

Luckily there was a little tin of wet cleansing pads in the bag, as well as powder and lipstick. She did what she could with her appearance, but it still wasn't very good. And she couldn't bear to let the others know that she had been crying.

She rose, brushed her dress with her hand and wandered on through the bushes and trees, catching her hair and once getting a stinging slap from a branch. It was a surprise when she suddenly came out on the drive, within a few yards of the big gates. Beyond the gates was the busy road, with the lake not far away and across the water rocky Monte Generoso rose up against the blazing sky.

Drina walked to the gates, filled with an almost overpowering desire to run away. Out there was freedom; people enjoying the September sun, able to do as they pleased.

She was beyond the gates, watching the cars flashing past, when there were footsteps behind her and she whirled round to see Madame Maréchel, with a small white poodle on a lead.

Madame approached her briskly.

"You're one of the new girls? Let me see – the dancer one. Drina Adams. What are you doing out here?"

"Just – just looking, Madame."

"Well, my child, perhaps you don't yet know, but no girl is allowed out of the gates alone."

"I was only about two *yards* beyond the gates." The words came out defiantly, and Drina heard them with horror.

Madame flushed. She had noted the signs of tears and had been prepared to be sympathetic, but the brusque, almost impertinent tone annoyed her.

"You will not be one yard out, please. It is a strict rule. In fact, we do not encourage the girls to come down here at all. The grounds are large. There is tennis, clock golf, even a swimming-pool. You will at once return to the house, Miss Selby wishes to speak to all the girls at six o'clock."

"Yes, Madame. I'm sorry." Drina turned and obeyed, fuming at herself and Madame. She had behaved stupidly, but then the rules were stupid. Everything was stupid! She felt so totally "all wrong" that she could not see how she was ever to be "all right". And it was humiliating, when she was used to be being treated as a reasonable human being by most people, to be regarded as a rude child.

Madame Maréchel, whose poodle Mimi was always upset by the excitements of the first day of term, walked her pet slowly up the drive in Drina's wake. She shut Mimi in the staff sitting-room and went to tell Miss Selby of the little incident, following closely after Miss Green, who had overheard the lunch-time conversation about boys and who had decided, after cogitation, that she had better report it. The staff had been asked to be vigilant after the dreadful affair of the elopement, which might easily have ruined the school.

Thus, on that first afternoon, Drina began to acquire a reputation for being "difficult".

The next evening Drina sat on the window-seat of one of the girls' sitting-rooms, writing to Rose. Around her was music and chatter, but she did not hear any of it.

Dear Rose,

Well, here I am and it's almost unbelievably awful. Milan, of course, was marvellous, and the glimpses I had of the Ticino looked heavenly, but here I'm behind high walls, forbidden to go one yard out of the gates. Oh, I went shopping this afternoon with about ten others, but we had two of the staff with us. I can't tell you how being carefully chaperoned tries me; it brings out my very worst nature. I've lectured myself, but it doesn't do much good. The others grumble and laugh about it, but they've nearly all been to some kind of boarding-school immediately before coming here, so I suppose it comes more naturally to them.

We were ten times more free at Chalk Green. Of course that was in the country and Lugano is quite a big town and still crowded with holiday-makers, but it still seems silly. Bianca got talking to a young man in the chemist's shop, where she went to buy some toothpaste – she had come without any – and Madame was quite annoyed with her.

They are all very silly about boys and young men, but I'm sure this way of life makes them worse. It's exciting to snatch a chance, even of talking to a young chemist. I learned later that Bianca forgot the toothpaste on purpose, because she admires him. Goodness me! I don't know what they'd make of the Dominick and us all rubbing shoulders all the time. This place is out of the ark – incredible!

The house is lovely and so are the gardens, but I'm conscious of the wall and the gates – closed now that everyone has arrived. We are to bathe tomorrow in the lovely little green-blue pool, and the sun is pure heaven, but I feel as though I shall never get used to being here.

This morning I put on my practice costume and worked alone for an hour. I worked hard, but I didn't enjoy it, it was so depressing to be alone. There is a piano and a record-player in the studio and piles of records. There's even a record of Twentieth Century Serenade. I did a bit of my ballet, but it made me feel so awful that I stopped.

The girls are nice, but they do seem to me rather silly. Yet maybe I'm being silly myself, and smug. I'm sure we're all frivolous sometimes, but they seem to be all the time. It's mainly that the atmosphere is so different from the Dominick, where everyone works as though they mean it, and there's always a shade of anxiety.

They have mostly been very friendly and they ask questions about the Dominick and the plays I've been in, and though I honestly didn't deliberately try to impress them they do seem impressed because I know actors and dancers. Most of them have heard of Catherine Colby and Renée Randall. Not to mention Peter Bernoise.

But the staff aren't impressed with me at all. I worked badly today, I'm afraid, and Madame Maréchel, for one, doesn't like me. Miss Selby is a typical school-marm: rather earnest and with very little sense of humour, I feel sure. She hasn't a notion about ballet. She came into the studio while I was still practising and said:

"Very nice, dear. Do you know anything pretty that you could dance at our end-of-term concert?"

I nearly spat in her eye. I'm not a lady. Goodness, I don't think I suffer from a swelled head, but that I should descend to that!

I don't think she liked my look. I was too speechless to answer. I shouldn't mind dancing at their awful concert, really; it was her tone.

I think of the Dominick constantly. What I wouldn't give to have lunch in the canteen instead of in this elegant, altogether delightful dining-room. I even think with nostalgia of the smelly old cloakroom: sweat and old shoes and stale make-up! Everything here is bright and lovely, with flowers all over the place. And the view from my bedroom window is beautiful, but I'd give up the lot for one chance to walk along Kingsway.

Yes, I'm grumbling and I vowed I wouldn't. In many, many ways I'm ashamed of myself, but I never thought it would be as bad as this. The whole truth may be that I'm used, these days, to feeling a little important, and here I'm no one, really. Not to the staff. Not rich, and pretty, and not likely to make a wonderful marriage soon. You should see Francesca's ring. She comes from Rome and is beautiful. She also seems to have more brains than most of them, but of course she doesn't notice me much. She and a few others – including another Italian, Fiora, who is also engaged – are in a little clique, very grand and remote.

Write soon and tell Ilonka that she must too. Tell me all the news. I wonder who will play Jane? I don't see why it shouldn't be you. You can sing better than me and you look pretty young on the stage. Give my love to everyone who is interested, and don't tell Queenie and Sylvia that I'm miserable. Tell the dear girls that I'm having a wonderful time.

Yes, pride dies hard. In fact, it's keeping me going, but only just.

Love from Drina.

5

A Dancer
Misunderstood

On Friday morning there was a letter from Rose, for she had not waited to hear from Drina. She wrote cheerfully, putting in little scraps of news and gossip that she knew would interest Drina.

Igor asked me to go to a film with him the other evening. Just fancy! He's so grand these days that I know I ought to be highly flattered. So I put on my best bib and tucker and sallied forth to meet him. I must say he was at his best, but my poor mother wasn't at all keen about it. Remember that she once met Igor in London when he was at his very worst, silly and showing off. Mum likes Jan, but she really wishes I would make friends with some of the local boys. She doesn't hold with these "ballet boys", as she calls them. Anyway, Igor and I had quite a good time and the only snag was that he talked such a lot about you! You've made a hit there, anyone can see.

Queenie's mother – the once great Beryl Bertram, poor woman! – has been ill, it seems, and Queenie is rather subdued. Sylvia is not. She's heard all about The Land of Christmas and is determined to get a part.

A pipe burst in one of the cloakrooms and you never saw

such a mess. The staff are starting to say that the sooner we move to the new building the better. Somehow one does see now that the old Dominick is looking very shabby and tumbledown.

The weather has been just awful since you left. Rain every day. I think of you in sunshine amongst oranges and lemons and think I wouldn't mind a stay in Southern Switzerland. I've had a cold, but not really bad enough to stay away, thank goodness. Though Miss Lane heard me sneezing and said, "Rose, dear. I hope you're not spreading germs?"

Ilonka sends her love and says that she will be writing soon. Meryl turned her ankle going downstairs yesterday and was away today. Won't she be upset, right at the start of term? Oh, and Miss Volonaise met me yesterday in the square and said to send you her love if I was writing soon. Her love. Goodness! But then she did know your mother.

Don't fret too much. Some of it must be lovely. The view from my bedroom window is disgusting: beastly little gardens and wet grey roofs. I hate London.

Drina put the letter in her bag, tied her ballet shoes and went soberly down to her solitary practising. Crossing the glowing garden to the studio she paused to look at the flawless sky, at the wooded slopes of Monte San Salvatore towering above, and at a group of older girls – of which Francesca was the centre – crossing the lawn. Rose at Earls Court in a rather horrid little semi-detached house and herself here … and she would have abandoned it all without a backward glance.

She had never felt so alone in her life, so strangely without roots. She did not even feel in any way close to Antonia. Antonia, when they met in the bedroom or at meals, was still as friendly as ever, but Antonia had her own friends and actually enjoyed her school life. Antonia, Drina sensed, was baffled by her young

cousin's attitude to the school and it seemed little use
trying to explain.

Sighing, Drina looked through the records until she
came to one that would do, then went to the *barre* and
began to warm up. The number of mornings that she
must do this in solitude appalled her, but she set her
chin and tried to lose herself in hard work. There was
nothing else for it.

Signora Lerrani was expected in time for lunch and
Drina was to have her first lesson at two o'clock. She
changed back into her practice costume and returned to
the studio, expecting to be first, but already there was
someone there – a middle-aged woman, with curly
greying hair, fine features and a body that still
proclaimed that she had been a well-known dancer.

They eyed each other, Drina rather flushed, and then
Signora Lerrani said in Italian:

"You're Drina Adams? I know all about you. I know
Marianne Volonaise quite well. It's simply absurd
sending you to a place like this, but I must say I'm
grateful. These girls don't know the meaning of hard
work, though some of them have the makings of good
dancers."

"Then why –?" Drina stopped, biting her lip.

"Why do I trouble to travel from Milan to teach them?
Well, there are various reasons, and the chief of them is
that Miss Selby has a cousin by marriage who is one of
the administrators of La Scala. That surprises you? Poor
Celia Selby doesn't know the first thing about ballet, nor
about opera. But she wants the best for her school and
will go all out to get it. The girls are charged enormous
fees, too, for these lessons. Not you: I said I'd take you
for the minimum fee and be glad to, but don't tell
anyone. Then *I* have a dear sister who lives in Lugano

and it gives me great pleasure to see her twice a week before I go home. You are satisfied?'' Her lips twitched with amusement, and Drina, feeling as though she had met a fellow human being for the first time in this place, grinned back.

"Oh, Signora, you make me feel much better! None of them understand ... I feel so out of things. And – and –''

"You're a professional. It's inevitable that you feel lost here. But it's a pleasant place. Ah, here's Miss Green. She's going to play for us. Let's get to work; there's no time to waste.''

She did not, in fact, waste another minute, and Drina enjoyed the hour, after some initial nervousness. She was not used to being the sole object of attention and she was also conscious that she was rather out of practice. For she had not attended regular classes since July.

The others arrived at three – nine girls in all – and Drina ran away to shower and change before a French literature class in the shade of one of the big chestnuts. The stimulus of the ballet class stayed with her for quite a time, but by evening she was restless again and wishing most heartily that she had been allowed to go to the villa for the weekend. The very thought of freedom on so warm and still an evening filled her with longing. In just such autumn heat she had got to know New York. On warm May evenings in Paris she had been with Grant, when she wasn't dancing. Grant ... Would he ever write? She went rather rapidly indoors and, sitting curled up on her favourite window-seat, began to write to Miss Whiteway.

The weekend seemed to pass very slowly. The pleasantest thing was that Drina was included in a party of a dozen or so girls that was taken by funicular to the summit of San Salvatore on Saturday afternoon. It was another glorious day and the view from the top was so superb that for a time she quite forgot her troubles. The lake and the curving town lay far below, every detail clear, and the view extended for many miles to the glorious snow-peaks: Monte Rosa, the Matterhorn and many others.

Even so there was trouble in the end, for Drina wandered away from the group, entirely intent on the beauty about her, and it was sheer accident that she got mixed up with a jolly party of French holidaymakers. She inadvertently dropped her bag; it was picked up by a handsome young man, who bowed and made some courteous remark, and there was Madame Maréchel, looking as though it had all been done on purpose.

"Drina, you will please keep with the others. To drop the bag ... a vulgar old trick that. If not the bag, the handkerchief."

Drina was furious and narrowly bit back the words that it was Madame who was being vulgar. Though she was well aware that Bianca, for instance, might well have tried to attract the young Frenchman in such a way.

So the afternoon was spoilt, and Drina returned to the school in what passed for sulky silence. Though, really, she was only fully occupied with controlling her homesickness and misery.

Antonia thought it all a ridiculous fuss about nothing.

"Even if you did drop your bag on purpose ... what would it matter? And Madame is like that, silly old thing. You take it all too seriously."

"I can't help it, Antonia. I don't *do* things like that. I was – was just loving that glorious view, one of the loveliest I've ever seen. I'm just not used to being looked at with suspicion. I'm used to being *trusted*. And that young man *heard* what she said. I felt so humiliated."

"No one trusts us here," Antonia said lightly, in Italian. "Well, perhaps they trust Francesca and one or two of the other older ones. Francesca is already conscious of her future, but most of us are just on the look-out for fun. Drina, don't look like that. Can't you *laugh*?"

"No," said Drina hollowly, and it was true that her sense of humour seemed wholly to have left her. "I *hate* Madame! I could – could kick her teeth in." This in English.

"That is not *comme il faut*," said Antonia, grinning.

"And who cares? *I'm* not going to marry a diplomat. I'm going to spend half my life in theatrical digs in provincial towns. Oh, I want Rose! Rose would understand. Everyone at home would understand. I – I'm out of my depth and I think I shall drown." She rushed into her cubicle and drew the curtains with a savage rattle.

So the days passed slowly to Drina. She grew thinner in a very short time and when she went to the villa the following weekend Mrs Chester was privately much concerned. Drina was still deeply suntanned, but there were shadows under her eyes and her cheerfulness seemed forced.

"What's the matter with you?" Mrs Chester demanded, when she got her granddaughter alone. "Aren't you eating enough?"

"Oh, yes, Granny. The food's marvellous."

"Well, don't you like the school? Aren't you making friends? Antonia said they were such a nice lot of girls."

"It's all right." It was no use trying to explain. Besides, she had to some extent made her choice and must abide by it. "I'm not used to it yet. It's all so different. Different ways of working, you know."

"You're the youngest. Are the lessons too hard for you?"

"Oh, no, Granny. I can keep up. The languages are no trouble and I've read such a lot that it helps."

Mrs Chester shook her head, knowing that she was going to hear some remarks from her husband, but by the next day Drina looked better and even entertained them with portraits of the different girls and members of staff. She was a good mimic and some, especially Ethel Benkoff, came over vividly.

It was wonderful to sleep alone in her pretty room, wonderful to eat breakfast peacefully out on the terrace under the oleanders, and more wonderful still to go shopping with her grandmother and to escape alone, while Mrs Chester sat in the gardens by the lake, to explore the town. Passing the Museo Civico she saw a party of her schoolfriends just going in and Bianca hissed:

"*Alone*! Lucky girl! I wish *my* family would take a villa here. Heavens! There's Madame looking back! Yes, Madame, I am coming."

Madame thought it a great pity that the difficult Drina Adams should be able to leave the school at weekends. It was unsettling for the other girls to see her sauntering along unaccompanied.

Yes, Drina was, to most members of the staff, that "rather difficult, girl, Drina Adams". Much of this could not have been avoided, for tension and unhappiness had definitely made her unlike herself. In spite of her words to her grandmother she was not working as well as usual, because concentration seemed difficult, and most of the teachers thought of her as "unco-operative". She had a certain air that they found hard to define, as well. The youngest and the smallest, she might easily have been popular with girls and staff alike, but there was a sturdy independence about her, as well as a faint arrogance, that people like Madame Maréchel, and even Miss Marlow, found difficult to accept. The fact that Drina despised many things about the school she had not troubled to hide, and she had a way of looking when some rule was mentioned that was little short of impertinent. So many of them thought, anyway.

It was all most unfortunate, and Drina was self-conscious enough, and sensitive enough, to have a very good idea of where she had gone wrong. But she seemed powerless to get right with herself, and consequently she stayed "all wrong" with most aspects of her new world.

There was her dancing, too. The hour a day spent practising seemed to most of the teachers excessive and it surprised them that she showed not the slightest sign of wishing to cut it short. If anyone looked in she was working steadily and usually did not even notice their presence.

But Drina tried not to think of any of this during that weekend at the Villa Mimosa. The sun shone, she was free, and she made the most of it. On Sunday afternoon she and her grandparents went to Gandria and Drina was enchanted with the little coloured houses overhanging the lake. They had tea on a balcony above the water, watching small boats and occasional bigger ones go past.

But time passed all too rapidly and she had to be back at the school in time for supper.

Her grandfather got her alone just before she set off.

"Look, my dear, if you simply hate it we'll do something … I always knew we shouldn't uproot you from the Dominick, but your grandmother was so firm about bringing you and –"

Drina's eyes flew open in dismay. He was obviously so much better, and he just mustn't be worried or upset.

"Of course not, Grandfather. I'm quite all right. And now I must *fly*, or Miss Selby will be cross."

"And I bet she expects me to be escorted," she thought, as she darted through the gates and up the drive, where the shadows were already deep. It got dark early now that it was almost October.

Lights were already springing up in the house, but fortunately no one noticed her arrival until she had reported to Matron. A large party had been on a lake steamer that afternoon and everyone seemed in very high spirits.

When Drina had been at the school for two weeks Miss Selby invited her to her sitting-room and tried to have a friendly talk, but this was not very successful. Drina sensed strongly that they were incompatible and that she could never make Miss Selby understand, so she remained unresponsive. It seemed an awful position, so she did her best to look demure. Miss Selby, baffled and disturbed, soon dismissed her.

The girl was not actually badly behaved, in spite of the various small, disturbing incidents. She seemed to be trying to work and she was obviously of high intelligence. But she was an alien quantity. Unhappy, too, thought Celia Selby, with a sigh, and it was not usual for girls to be unhappy at her school. Little sisters often followed older girls ... cousins ... friends.

And Signora Lerrani spoke highly of her. But *she* came from an alien world, too. In her secret heart Miss Selby found the Italian ballet teacher a formidable and rather terrifying woman, and this was unusual, for she was not often intimidated. She liked to think that she could meet people of high importance if not on equal terms, then with poise and great dignity.

The girls, however, were still fascinated by Drina and many of them would have been glad to be friends. Occasionally she livened up and entertained them with stories of her dancing life, and these they found most amusing and astonishing. Bianca even worked much harder at ballet because she began to think it mightn't be a bad idea to turn into a real dancer. Bianca was one of the few who had learned ballet from a very early age and her technique was good. It was concentration that had been lacking.

"But my family would never agree," she said sadly to Drina. "I'm rich. Isn't it a bore? Do you *have* to work for your living?"

This was a point that had been puzzling many of them, for Drina seemed to lack nothing. Her clothes were nearly as good as theirs, occasionally better. The Paris dress was admired by all. And all her possessions were more than passable. She had travelled, too, and did not seem in any way poor. It was very bewildering.

"Well, I don't know," Drina said casually. "That hasn't really a lot to do with it. I've some money of my own – quite a lot, I think. I've just known all my life – well, since I was very young – that I had to be a dancer."

They had none of them really the least idea of what it meant to be dedicated to an art, but they respected her and did not resent the occasional calm airs of assurance. Even Francesca grew to be quite cordial.

Drina liked Ethel best, for they found the same things funny. Ethel was rich, too, but unlike the Italian and French girls she had not been chaperoned and she had no intention of marrying for anything but love. She had been around, was quite as independent as Drina, and found the rules almost equally irritating. But she could laugh at them, for she was casual and good-tempered. She was not very popular with the staff, for she had been a slightly disruptive element during the previous term, her first, and Ethel knew it but didn't care.

"I'm here to learn Italian and German and I'm learning both, so why worry? I want to be an interpreter. Oh, sure. I'm going to earn my living. Why not? Wall Street might crash at any time; anyway I'm not cut out for an idle life. I guess I need something to get my teeth in."

Yes, Drina liked her, but they had not really very much in common. Drina missed having a warm and intimate friend. Rose and Ilonka, as well as Jenny, were writing regularly, but they were far away.

Then, nearly three weeks after the beginning of term, she went up to her room to fetch a handkerchief and found the third cubicle occupied by a small, dark girl, who was sitting on the bed and contemplating a large green trunk.

Tamina Rionante had arrived.

6

Dancers in Berne

"**H**ullo!" said Tamina, in English. "You must be Drina Adams."

Her voice was soft and almost without accent, for she had spent nearly three years at the school in the Bernese Oberland where Miss Selby used to teach. She was very pretty in a rather delicate way and when she stood up she did so with extreme grace. She looked like a dancer.

"Yes, but how did you know?"

"Oh, Bianca wrote and told me about you. And I'm so glad to meet you. I looked you up in the ballet magazines – I take all the English ones – and I found a picture of you in Paris with Igor Dominick Junior and two other girls. 'Miss Drina Adams, who is dancing Little Clara in the Dominick production of *Casse Noisette*.' It must be wonderful to be famous."

"I'm not," said Drina, knowing that it was true. Real fame was still a very long way off. But, strangely, she suddenly felt more like her old self. She had taken an instant liking for Tamina; though she was much darker, she reminded her of Rose.

Matron came in then and Drina was forced to find a handkerchief and go off to her next study group, but she sat next to Tamina at tea, both talking hard. The others surveyed them in some astonishment, for Tamina was normally quiet and had seemed to most people shy. And there was Drina Adams, who so often ate her meals in silence, chattering away and even laughing.

It was simply that Drina and Tamina had recognised at once – by some nameless chemistry – that they would be friends. It was not that Tamina flattered Drina, after that first remark about being famous. It was just that they had slipped, by the end of the day, into the comfortable awareness that they would understand each other. They came from alien backgrounds in different countries, but there it was.

"It must be because their names are alike," said Bianca, a little sore, because she would have liked Drina for a friend. "My friend, the famous ballet dancer" would have sounded well one day; in any case Bianca, a shallow but quite warm-hearted girl, liked Drina for herself.

"I don't know what it is," said Antonia, the next day, "but you would think they had known each other all their lives." She was an easy-going girl, and was extremely relieved that Drina had cheered up, but she was vaguely conscious of being out of things in the bedroom now that Tamina occupied the third cubicle.

Tamina and Drina, both sensitive, were very soon aware of this and did their best to include her in all their conversations, but there were territories into which Antonia could not follow them. Tamina was a reader, where Antonia never willingly looked at a book in any language. Tamina loved the ballet and knew a great deal about it, though she had not seen very many professional performances; also she was musical and was learning the violin. Drina, after the arrival of Tamina, spent much more time playing the piano and sometimes they played together. Drina was supposed to keep up her music, and was to have lessons as soon as the visiting music master, who took the more advanced pupils, recovered from an illness, but she had been neglecting her practising, where she had stuck so grimly to her hour of ballet.

By the time Tamina had been at school three days they knew a good deal about each other, though Tamina did not know that Elizabeth Ivory – whose memory she seemed greatly to revere – had been Drina's mother. Tamina read the lives of ballet dancers whenever she could lay hands on them, as well as poetry and plays.

"Before, there was no one to talk to about such things," she said, as she and Drina sat under the golden-brown leaves of the biggest chestnut tree.

Tamina had learned ballet for some years until she went to school in the Oberland and had been lucky in her teacher, who had retired to Locarno and taken just a few chosen pupils.

"I loved it," said Tamina, "and didn't mind how hard I worked. But Mother didn't think it mattered that I went to a school where I could not continue to learn. Madame Lerrani says that I've wasted years, though I did sometimes practise and have lessons in the holidays."

"Didn't you ever think of making it your career?"

"Oh, yes, often. I used to dream about it. But of course I never shall. For that one needs to go to a ballet school, like you."

Tamina lived in a villa near the shores of Lake Maggiore and had a little sister called Carla. It was not very far away and she, too, went home most weekends.

The friendship was observed with varying degrees of approval by the staff. Tamina had struck no one as a rebel and it was, on the whole, thought to be a good thing.

"I don't like such close friendships as a rule," said Miss Selby to Miss Marlow, "and Tamina has always struck me as a trifle weak. She is a charming girl, and clever, but easily influenced, I suspect. This friendship is so sudden that it seems unlikely to last, but Drina certainly seems happier."

Miss Selby thought that she herself had plenty of friends, but she had never felt any particularly strong affinity with anyone, man or woman. And she had not the slightest idea that Drina had been starved for lack of lively talk about the things that interested her, and for the ordinary warm sympathy that an understanding friend can give.

Drina *was* very much happier after the arrival of Tamina, but she was still by no means resigned to her exile in Lugano. Many times a day her thoughts flew to the Dominick and letters were one of the most important things in her life. And, as the weeks passed, she received an enormous number; far more than most of the other girls. Apart from Rose, Ilonka and Jenny, Adele Whiteway also wrote faithfully, and at different times there were letters from others in Drina's class at the Dominick: Meryl, the twins, Betty and Lorna. Hildegarde wrote from Germany, telling of her experiences at the Munich dancing school, which she attended all week, returning home to Dinkelsbühl for weekends. And Yolande Mason wrote from New York, telling of her dancing and other matters that she knew would interest Drina.

Manhattan is looking very beautiful, wrote Yolande early in October. *Rather as it looked when you were here last year.*

The leaves are falling in Washington Square and the mornings are sometimes misty. Yesterday my aunt and I went up to the Cloisters and it was just lovely on the ramparts, looking across the Hudson River. The woods are all gold and it was very hot. People are still wearing summer clothes, but winter will come soon now.

We are all getting kind of excited about the Christmas Performance, and Madame will soon be choosing who is to dance. She says she is very pleased with me. How you must miss the Dominick, and it does seem hard about the movie and the play.

Yolande felt that she owed Drina a great debt, for through Drina she had regained her confidence as a dancer. She was very happy now with her Aunt Grace, in the charming little house in Greenwich Village, and she never failed to send copies of the *New Yorker*, a magazine that Drina read from cover to cover, even the advertisements.

Drina always read Yolande's letters several times, too, especially for the bits about Manhattan. Every time she saw an American stamp she hoped that the letter might be from Grant, but this was never the case. To hear from Yolande was, however, a lot better than nothing.

Rose wrote every week without fail, and her letters were always chatty and informative.

Things are getting to boiling point one way and another, she wrote, about the middle of October. *What with the Dominick matinée and* The Land of Christmas *we're all ready to tear each other's eyes out. Sometimes I loathe this feeling of desperate rivalry. Keep it under your hat, but Miss Volonaise told me privately that they are going to audition me for Jane. I feel bad about it in some ways, for it ought to be you, but if it comes off I shall be so thrilled and so will Dad and*

Mum. It will mean earning good money for at least three weeks – it's to be a limited run, as it was last year –, and, though I should be terribly scared, it would be exciting as well and a step in my career, as Jane has such a lot of dancing.

The weather is still really horrible. I plod my way into Red Lion Square through the puddles, and we haven't even the pleasure of seeing the Company leaving the rehearsal rooms just now, because they've flown off to Moscow. Can you imagine that we'll ever dance at the Bolshoi?

Tamina sounds nice; I'm really glad that you've found a friend and flattered that you think she's like me. I can't believe that I really look like a rich Italian-Swiss. I'm not jealous, because I know you'll never forget your old friends, but I do miss you "something shocking". In some ways things are dismal, what with the weather, and I've had another cold and feel so tired, and they've been on at me again about my diet. I can't make Mum see that I oughtn't to eat so many fried things; she firmly believes they're nourishing and is very easily hurt. Sometimes I think very longingly of having a little flat of my own, though I always feel guilty. I'm fond of the kids, but they're a menace. I just can't get my homework done in peace.

Then, obviously determined not to end on an unhappy note, Rose went on to tell about the boy who had come to live next door and who was doing his best to go out with her. Rose always seemed vividly near as Drina read her letters.

Puddles and colds and a fattening diet did sound depressing things, but Drina envied Rose quite fiercely even as she looked out at the lake, the golden vineyards and the trees with bright leaves still clinging to them. It was cooler in the Ticino now, for the most part, but there were still lovely days when the sun shone. After one such day, when she had been to Morcote, Drina wrote back to her friend.

I envy you – I truly do, though my diet is just wonderful. I hope you get Jane – I don't see why you shouldn't. And I did laugh over the boy next door, poor thing. Don't be too unkind to him, even if he can't compete with Igor. But oughtn't you to confess about feeling so tired? It can't be right to feel like that.

I'm not doing my ballet practising alone now. Not every day, anyway. Signora Lerrani suggested that Tamina and Bianca might practise with me, and I was so sick of being alone that I agreed. They work hard and it certainly makes it more stimulating. My ordinary work is going better, too; I gritted my teeth and got down to it. But there's an awful lot about this place that still drives me mad, and sometimes I think I'll break out and do something outrageous. It is the feeling of being shut in. Of course, in actual fact, we go out a lot, but always with at least one member of staff and usually two. And when it's Madame she always looks at me as though she expects me to misbehave.

One afternoon recently we had a private bus and went to Bellinzona, and in some ways it was absolutely wonderful. It is a fascinating town, very Italian, with some narrow streets and stone arcades, and there are three castles on the hills. The top one is very high above the vineyards and Tamina, Bianca and I gave Miss Green and Madame no peace until they agreed to let us go. Madame was suffering from her feet – she wears heels like stilts – but Miss Green is energetic enough, so up we went. Grey rocks and golden vines – most of the grapes are gathered now – and the most lovely views of the valley, the higher mountains and little coloured churches perched on crags. And, up there, I escaped from the others and danced. No one saw me, and I do love to dance in the open air, in some lovely place. The last time was in Gibraltar in the Alameda Gardens, and then Jasper saw me, though I didn't mean him to. Miss Green asked where I'd been, when I went back to the others in the courtyard, but she didn't seem very interested. There were no young men up there! No one at all but us.

Then today we went to Morcote and it is a dream of a place, on Lake Lugano, with coloured boats in a little harbour, and more arcades, and a high, high church. Again poor Miss Green had to climb up all the hundreds of steps with us, and she did her best to make it educational by making us look at the church, which is very ornate, like so many here. But the nicest part was the terrace and the cypresses and the vast view of the lake and the mountains.

Since I came here small parties of girls have gone to Milan, Berne and Zurich, but it's mostly at weekends, and that's when I go home. They make quite a point of taking us around, but it's really no fun unless you can explore alone. In some ways I'm very much the Cat that Walked by Himself, as you know.

Last weekend Tamina's family were away, so she was allowed, after much fussing and telephoning, to come to the Villa Mimosa with me. I felt rather mean about Antonia, but there's no doubt that we've grown apart. Of course we never knew each other very well: just those days in Genoa and then the time when she came to England. She's nice, and lively, but now I think we both realise that we have very little in common.

Let me know about Jane just as soon as you know yourself. I suppose rehearsals will start early in December. I feel sick with longing sometimes just for the smell of a theatre, as you can imagine. There goes the bell for bed! Must fly.

Love,
Drina.

A week later Mrs Chester wrote to Drina to tell her that she and Mr Chester had been invited to Genoa for a long weekend and thought they had better go, so as not to hurt the Gardinos again. So Drina, of course, could not go to the villa. Mrs Chester went on to say that perhaps it would be a good idea if Drina joined one of the travelling parties, as she had not seen very much of Switzerland, and she intended to telephone Miss Selby and suggest it.

Drina would greatly have preferred to go home with Tamina, but before she could try and arrange an invitation she was called to Miss Selby's room and told that she was to go on tour for a long weekend, spending the Friday night at Lucerne, then seeing Thun and spending a couple of nights in Berne. There would be ten girls in the party, in the charge of Madame Maréchel and a young Swiss who taught German.

Fraülein Reichenbach was nice, but the thought of spending a weekend with Madame was anything but appealing. Even the chance to see Thun and Berne would not be worth it. However, it seemed too late to try to evade the trip and Drina's name was added to the list.

On the Friday that they were to leave Drina went to look for letters, as usual. These were always laid out in alphabetical order on the table in the hall. Hers were always easy to find, as she was the only girl in the school whose surname began with "A". There was one from Miss Whiteway on top, then one from Ilonka, and – Drina's heart leaped sickeningly – an airmail envelope with an American stamp. Her name and address were written in a bold hand that she knew at a glance, without the fact that, in the top left-hand corner, was also written: "From: Grant Rossiter, Central Park West, New York, 10023 N.Y."

Grant had written at last!

Then she saw that the envelope had been opened and the flap just left loose, with no attempt to stick it back again. For a moment she thought that Customs officials somewhere had opened it; then she realised that, in that case, it would certainly have been resealed and probably stamped.

Her long-buried temper flared out suddenly. A letter from Grant – a precious letter, a private letter – and someone had dared to open it. Her cheeks very red, the letter held against her chest, she spun round and found Madame Maréchel standing there, glancing at a newspaper.

Fury overrode all discretion. She said:

"Madame, someone has opened my private letter!"

Madame Maréchel glanced from her angry face to the letter that was suddenly thrust out. She had long sight and no need of glasses.

"Miss Selby looks at all the letters. Occasionally she opens one. That, I see, is from a man."

"But – but it's outrageous! In my whole life –"

Madame promptly marched her to Miss Selby, and by the time they arrived in the study Drina was calmer; common sense had intervened. The more of a scene that she made the more attention would be drawn to Grant.

Miss Selby waited until they were alone, then said quietly:

"Drina, it says in the prospectus that I reserve the right to open letters. I tried to get hold of your grandmother, to ask if you were allowed to receive letters from this Grant Rossiter, but they must have left for Genoa."

"They went yesterday afternoon. I am. Of course I am, Miss Selby. He's a – a family friend."

"Well, then it seems a great fuss over what is only a short note. Run along and get on with your ballet practice. Oh, and *do* remember to wear warm clothes and strong shoes to go to Berne. It will be much colder in the North."

"And even if she does think a lot of that young man he's too far away to cause any trouble," she said to herself, as Drina, without another word, closed the door quietly behind her.

Drina rushed off towards the studio, but met Tamina on the way. Tamina took one look at her friend's face and asked:

"What's the matter? Has something awful happened?"

"I suppose not, but it seems awful to me; an – an invasion of privacy. Miss S-Selby opened a letter from Grant." Tamina had heard a little about Grant and was at once sympathetic.

"Oh, that is awful of her, but she *will* do it. She once opened a letter from one of my boy cousins. But Grant has written, Drina. That should make you happy."

"Well, it does. But I hate to think –" And Drina, as the nine o'clock bell rang, went on to the studio, shut the door firmly on the outside world, and, leaning against the piano, read Grant's note.

There was certainly nothing in it that could have upset Miss Selby, beyond the fact that he seemed deeply to sympathise with her for being in "exile". He had been working hard at his job in his father's office, but he had found time to go to see the New York City Ballet and to a much-praised new play. He still hoped that maybe he would be working in London next year and held her to her promise of going with him to the Royal Opera House. He ended, in his usual way: "My best, always."

In London, some day, they would meet again. That thought was a comfort, but all the same Drina felt more "all wrong" than usual for the rest of the day. She got ready for the weekend trip in gloomy silence and spent a good part of the journey to Lucerne standing in the train corridor. Bianca, who was in the group, did her best to make her talk, but didn't suceed. Also in the party were Lotti, who learned ballet and was rather nice, and a lovely young Greek girl who had been new with Drina, but whom she had never got to know, beyond the exchange of a few polite words.

Once through the Gotthard tunnel there was far more snow on the mountains than when Drina had travelled south in September and the sky was grey. The heating immediately increased on the train and suddenly it was really winter.

"We are unlucky," said Madame gloomily, for she did not like the cold. "So early in the year and already there has been snow. Only on the peaks, but still – Bianca, I beg of you not to giggle like that. Behave like a young lady and not like a silly schoolgirl."

It was dark long before they reached Lucerne and they went at once to their hotel. After dinner Madame decreed bed for everyone and an early start the next morning to look at the old town, before catching the train for Thun. Drina was still in low spirits, for once not very interested in new scenes, but she cheered up a little as, later in the day, they sped from Interlaken along the shores of the Thunersee. Up there in the mountains was Kandersteg.

"If it were summer we would have sailed up the lake," said Fraülein Reichenbach, who came from Spiez and wished that she could pay a quick visit to her home.

Thun, with its high, romantic-looking Schloss and old streets, was very fascinating, and, seeing the two rows of shops, one above the other with a walk high above street level, Drina was nostalgically reminded of Francaster, where she had spent Christmas last year. It was strange to meet the same unusual architectural feature here in Switzerland.

But the afternoon turned bitterly cold and there was a heavy rainstorm that drove them early to the station. The rain had stopped when they reached Berne and Madame said that it was not far to their hotel in the Spitalgasse. It was just as they were leaving the station that Drina glanced idly at a poster and stiffened with shock and amazement. For the words "Lingeraux Ballet Company" had leaped out at her. No one noticed – for she was one of the last – when she paused to take in the astonishing news. The Lingeraux Company was dancing at the Stadt-Theater for a week, starting on the following Monday.

She followed the others dazedly into the streets of Berne, with no eyes for the delightful grey-gold buildings and russet roofs. The Lingeraux! Madame Lingeraux, then, and Carol Collingwood and Jasper. He had never mentioned Berne; perhaps it was an extra booking, since they were to be in Basle and Zurich, anyway. Suddenly nothing was real but her old life, and get to the Stadt-Theater she must!

Not this evening, obviously. There would be something else on then, but probably the company would arrive tomorrow. There might even be a rehearsal. If they were only travelling from Basle they might do so after the show tonight, or at any rate early in the morning.

The hotel was old, delightfully warm, and smelling of polish. And, as luck would have it, it was not full and there were some single rooms available. Most of the girls preferred to share, so Drina got one without difficulty. This was so unexpected that she cheered up even more and greatly enjoyed her dinner. Though while she ate she was wondering how on earth to manage to make her escape the next day. She was still puzzling over this when they set off, in taxis, for the Kursaal, where Miss Selby had taken tickets for a good concert.

The concert was rather wasted on Drina, for she could not get the thought of her ballet friends out of her mind. Nothing, *nothing* was going to stand in the way of her seeing them. She did, for a moment, wonder if the simplest way would not be to ask permission, but it was fairly certain that Madame Maréchel would not give it.

Drina dreamed confusedly about ballet that night and awoke to a bright Sunday morning with her mind still made up. Trouble or not, she was going to find the Lingeraux. It was no very great crime, after all, and by the next morning she would be speeding back to the Ticino.

As she dressed she whistled to herself, sure that she would find an opportunity. Life had not seemed so worth living for quite a time.

7

A Ballet for Christmas

Only the Catholics and Madame went to church and this they did before breakfast. Immediately after breakfast Madame gathered the whole party together and said that they would now explore Berne. Fraülein Reichenbach distributed some little street maps of the city – which was a bonus for Drina because the Stadt-Theater was marked – and told them of some of the famous fountains they would see, the Clock Tower, the Town Hall and the Cathedral, with the ancient streets around it.

"And the bear-pits!" cried Bianca, who found architecture very boring. She had absolutely no feeling for history.

"The bear-pits also," agreed Fraülein Reichenbach, who did not greatly care for this most famous sight. *She* adored history and old buildings and she had been to college in Berne.

"And, of course, the Parliament Building and the terrace with a view," said Madame. She was privately wondering why on earth she allowed herself to be allocated to these wretched educational trips, especially on a morning that, though sunny, was disgustingly cold for early November. In deference to the ancient cobblestones of Berne she wore rather lower heels than usual, but she was no great walker at the best of times and also she suspected that she would have a headache later.

"This afternoon we will visit the Art Galleries and maybe the Alpine Museum," she said gloomily, as Fraülein Reichenbach led the way along the Spitalgasse.

Now that her mind was made up, Drina's spirits remained high and the magic of Berne soon exerted itself. She vowed that she would enjoy the city that morning and make her escape in the afternoon, when there would be more chance of the Company being at the theatre. It ought to be quite easy to slip out of one of the galleries.

It was such a sparklingly clear morning that the view of the Alps from the terrace behind the Parliament Building was superb, and, as they walked on into the more ancient streets, where the uneven houses lined the narrow, cobbled ways, the light brought out the glow of the old stone. Almost everything was a delight to the eye and, since she could not be alone, Drina attached herself to Fraülein Reichenbach and asked such intelligent, interested questions that Madame, overhearing, was quite amazed.

They returned to the hotel for lunch and afterwards the threatened headache, quite apart from the ache in her poor arches, was overwhelming Madame Maréchel. She accompanied them to the first Art Gallery, remarking on the way that there was an unexpectedly fine collection of early French Impressionists and Post Impressionists. Drina, who loved French art, could not bear to miss seeing these pictures, even though she so longed to find her friends.

And luck was with her, later, because Madame, having survived the Kunstmuseum and usually so conscientious, announced that she thought she would return to the hotel and take some aspirin for her headache. The party went on to the other gallery, some distance away on the far side of the river, actually passing the Stadt-Theater on the way. It was as much as Drina could do not to try and escape then and there, especially as she could see scenery being unloaded, but she went on, knowing that a good opportunity would come. And it did, because Fraülein Reichenbach was annoyed with Madame for evading her duties and so was consequently less vigilant than she was expected to be. She said that they could all separate when they reached the gallery and assemble again by the main door in an hour.

Drina gave them all time to disperse, evading Bianca, and simply walked out again, then ran as fast as she could to the theatre. Hurrying to where she thought the stage door might be, she saw a group ahead, and they were so unmistakably ballet dancers – anoraks, scarves and cases or holdalls – that her heart leaped with triumph. That dark head – that was Jasper, and in front of the men was a girl with fair hair. Carol!

Drina shouted and they all turned round. Jasper shouted in his turn and then he and Carol came running, laughing and astonished.

"*Drina*! Where have you come from? We thought you were in Lugano!"

"I was. I mean – it's an educational journey. I've escaped … I saw the advertisements … I should be looking at pictures. They guard us like – like –"

"But this is marvellous!" Jasper seized her arm and Carol took the other side. "Come and tell us all about it. You look thinner. Your cheeks are quite hollow. You never wrote," he said, in a lower voice.

"I know. I'm sorry. There isn't a lot of time."

"But what's it like? That school."

"Awful," said Drina. "Awful for me. I miss everything and everyone so dreadfully, and they *do* open letters, and – oh, I get so mad. Then there's *The Land of Christmas* and not being Jane. I *have* tried to like it, but it doesn't really work. What are you going to do now? Rehearse?"

"No. We're just bringing our stuff and coming to have a look. We rehearse tomorrow morning. This was an extra date, fitted in. We've never danced here before. Madame ought to be around somewhere. She'll want to see you."

They hauled Drina into the theatre and at once she breathed the beloved smell – theatres smelt the same all over the world – and there was Madame Lingeraux, on a nearly bare stage. She was a small and ugly woman, but just then she seemed beautiful to Drina.

"My dear child! Where have you come from?"

"I'm staying here, Madame. Just till tomorrow. With a school party. Isn't it the most wonderful coincidence? Oh, I have *missed* everything so!"

Madame Lingeraux eyed her shrewdly, noting that she was certainly thinner and obviously not very happy. Madame Lingeraux knew about Elizabeth Ivory and had been highly pleased to have Drina dance with her company in Madeira. She still remembered that hot and beautiful evening when Drina had last danced her own ballet in the little open-air theatre in Funchal. That night there had been a touch of great dancing and it seemed criminal to remove the girl from her proper environment and incarcerate her in a Swiss finishing school.

"Getting some dancing, are you? Not neglecting it altogether?"

"Oh, Madame, no. I practise every day and have lessons twice a week from Signora Lerrani, who comes from Milan. But it's not like being at the Dominick."

"Have you planned any new ballets lately?"

"No-o. There doesn't seem any point. But there's been one at the back of my mind for a long time. I call it *New York Rhapsody* and it goes to the New World Symphony."

"There have been other ballets to the New World, but that doesn't matter. One day I'll hope to see it. Bless me! I wish *I'd* got you!" said Madame Lingeraux. They were standing a little apart.

Drina flushed with pleasure.

"Oh, Madame! I'm – I'm nothing very much."

"Rubbish! The Dominick people are lucky. Get that ballet done – in your head, if nowhere else."

Jasper and Carol claimed her again then and they sat in the darkened auditorium, exchanging news and views. Drina never even thought about the time and her heart leaped sickeningly when she glanced at her watch. The hour was already almost up.

"I must go! There'll be an awful row if I'm discovered. I –"

"Rubbish!" said Jasper. "You can't rush away when we haven't met for such a long time. Well, why not meet us after dinner tonight? We're staying at the –"

"I can't. I *wish* I could, but Madame Maréchel would never agree."

"Then we'll come to your hotel. *I* will."

But now Drina was fully realising that her friends would never be acceptable to Madame Maréchel.

"It's no good, honestly. And I *have* seen you and been in a theatre again. I feel better now. I really must fly!"

Jasper was on his feet, too.

"I'm coming with you."

And he could not be shaken from this intention. There was no time to argue, so Drina set off with him. Leaving the theatre they met Cécile Barreux, the prima ballerina of the company, and she greeted Drina with flattering warmth. It was impossible to break away for nearly five minutes, and then Drina began to run.

"Jasper, I wish you wouldn't … I'm really late and Fraülein will be looking for me. It will make it worse if –"

"Tell her your grandmother knows me and it's quite all right," said Jasper, hurrying beside her. He felt he couldn't bear to lose her yet, this pale, unusually thin-faced girl who never quite left his thoughts.

They crossed the bridge and there, outside the gallery, was a little knot of girls, with Fraülein Reichenbach looking frantically up and down. She saw Drina and hurried towards her, her plain cheeks red with annoyance.

"Drina! We had them search the building and you – Where *have* you been?"

"To see my friends," Drina answered in English, though she had been addressed in German. She suddenly felt defiant; it was so absurd to be treated as a criminal. "They're dancing at the theatre here next week. The Lingeraux Ballet Company, you know. And this – this is Jasper."

Jasper said "How do you do?" and, with unusual formality, even bowed slightly. The girls, delighted by this unexpected occurrence, stared at him appreciatively, for he was rather a handsome young man.

Fraülein Reichenbach looked back at him helplessly and Jasper went on:

"I'm an old friend of Drina's. Her grandmother knows me. My name is Jasper Blane."

A ballet dancer! Not suitable at all, even though he seemed to have good manners, and who was to know that he was speaking the truth? In any case Drina Adams had been very wicked to sneak away.

"That may be so, but Drina is not supposed to run away to meet *anyone*. Come at once, girls. We will now return to the hotel. I don't know what Madame will say." She took Drina by the arm, signalled to the others to follow and away they went, leaving Jasper standing on the pavement. Some of the others looked back to smile and even wave, but Drina did not. She was seething.

Oh, idiot not to remember the time! It was, after all, so undignified to be marched back like a naughty child. And poor Jasper, being snubbed. But if he had stayed at the theatre it would have been easier. She found that part of her annoyance was that she had been treated as a child in front of an admirer.

There was, of course, an incredible row. Madame Maréchel knew herself at fault for yielding to her headache and tired feet; she knew also that Fräulein Reichenbach had been at fault for allowing the girls to separate. Her anger was therefore all the greater when she faced the silent, mulish-looking Drina Adams in the privacy of her own hotel room.

"This is disgraceful behaviour. So underhand. And to come back so blatantly with the young man –"

"He insisted on coming. And I wouldn't have been underhand, Madame, if I'd thought you would let me visit my friends. I – I *had* to see them. You don't understand ... ballet is my life. My grandmother does know Jasper. I had dinner with him just before we left London."

"Alone?" Madame threw up her hands.

"Yes. In England girls go out with young men when

they're quite young. There's – there's nothing *wrong* in it. It's quite usual and natural."

"But you are in our charge. And barely sixteen. I shall have to tell Miss Selby and she'll be most distressed. I always knew you were a troublesome girl."

"I've never been troublesome before. It's this – this idiotic school!"

"Say no more. You had better retire to your room and go to bed at once. I will have some dinner sent up to you."

Drina obeyed. She was badly shaken now, for her grandmother would probably hear all about it, and there was – she suddenly realised – the danger that Miss Selby would ask her to leave the school. And that could not happen because of her grandfather.

They left Berne very early on Monday morning to make the long journey back to the Ticino. Drina was aware that she was something of a heroine to the girls, who would nearly all have liked to escape and enjoy themselves, but she was certainly very deeply in the two adults' bad books. Back at school, she was soon sent for by Miss Selby, leaving a startled and rather unhappy Tamina, who had only had time to hear part of the story. Tamina was afraid that she was going to lose her friend.

Miss Selby was grave, but not, apparently, quite as upset as Drina had expected.

"It was a very foolish thing to do and quite naturally Madame and Fraülein were very much disturbed. If you had asked your grandmother before you left here it might have been possible for your friends to visit you at the hotel. I have just spoken to her on the telephone and she assures me that she knows this Jasper Blane."

"But I didn't *know* they'd be in Berne, Miss Selby. I just saw the advertisements and –"

Miss Selby sighed, wishing more than ever that she had not accepted this young girl who was so besotted with the ballet world. She had been prepared to be very much annoyed, but something about Mrs Chester's calm tones and ready acknowledgement of Drina's friends in the Lingeraux Company had made her feel that perhaps the whole affair was not as serious as had been made out. Not that she would ever agree to Drina Adams joining any more travelling parties.

"Well, your grandmother wishes you to telephone her. You may do so now from the office."

Little more was said, and Drina thankfully escaped to speak to her grandmother. Mrs Chester was brief and to the point.

"I did what I could for you, Drina, and it really does seem to be rather a fuss. Of course you were wrong to be so underhand, but *I* can understand, where your teachers can't, that it must have been an overwhelming temptation. You must obey the rules of the school."

"I know, Granny. I do try. But when they were *there* –"

"Well, we'll say no more about it, and I doubt if Miss Selby will. Your grandfather sends his love and so do the Gardinos. You must bring Antonia home one weekend."

"Yes, I will. Thank you for – for being so understanding."

"I do my best," said Mrs Chester dryly. "Though you don't credit me with much imagination."

"Madame Lingeraux said she wished *she'd* got me."

"She doesn't know her luck," retorted her grandmother.

"She meant because of my *dancing*, not because of my sweet nature."

"All right. I didn't mean it. *I* wouldn't lose you, and

neither would the Dominick for long, you can rest assured of that. Goodbye."

Drina went dazedly back to Tamina, who was waiting anxiously. It was most unlike her grandmother to make a remark that verged on the sentimental. Even when you thought you knew people they could still surprise you.

So the whole affair died down and was not mentioned again, except by some of the girls who had been there. But Drina still felt sore, partly because she *had* behaved rather stupidly in some ways.

She threw herself into her ballet practising with extra vigour, to try and keep her thoughts at bay, and was in the studio on Wednesday afternoon some time before Signora Lerrani could be expected. Remembering Madame Lingeraux's words, she had been thinking a good deal about *New York Rhapsody* and this seemed a good opportunity to plan some of the choreography.

She put on the first movement of the New World Symphony and stood tapping her foot, her brow creased in thought. A backcloth of midtown skyscrapers as seen from Central Park. Lots of different people in the park: a young man and his girl … a group of Puerto Ricans, perhaps … children playing with a huge coloured ball … a handsome young man alone … mothers wheeling prams. As much as possible of the changing panorama of the park on a fine day.

And the young girl would have a solo to attract all eyes, and especially the eyes of the Stranger. Something like this. Drina waited for the start of the second movement, on the same side of the long-playing record, and then soon began to dance.

She was so totally absorbed that she did not hear the door open and it was a tremendous shock when Signora Lerrani said:

A Ballet for Christmas

"Very nice. Very interesting choreography. I've never seen that solo before."

"You – you couldn't, Signora. I've just made it up," Drina stopped a trifle breathlessly and turned off the record player.

"You – made – it – up? Heavens! But of course I remember. Marianne Volonaise mentioned a little ballet that you choreographed." Signora Lerrani walked to the piano and sat down on the stool.

"I come expecting you to be sad, because of all this trouble in Berne that I hear about. Ridiculous of them: they might know that you'd want to see your friends in the ballet. And here you are making a ballet of your own, and to such ambitious music. The name of it? Or don't you know?"

"Oh, yes. It's called *New York Rhapsody*. In Central Park, you know. That was the young girl's dance. I've just been thinking … Puerto Ricans and children and women with prams. And a handsome stranger who tries to steal a young man's girl. With a backcloth of skyscrapers and trees and maybe a bit of one of the lakes. But," said Drina, suddenly depressed, "what's the good of it?"

"I will tell you. You'll do this for Christmas here. They invite as many parents as possible to see the school, there's a buffet supper and displays of art work and so on. Last year some did a French play, and a few of my pupils danced. This year – *New York Rhapsody*."

"But, Signora –"

"I'll speak to Miss Selby. She is a little afraid of me." And she grinned. "You'll plan the ballet, and you will also design the set. I'm sure you can do that."

"Oh, I expect so. I've often seen my friend Adele Whiteway's designs and I'm not bad at art. But –"

"Then you will give orders to the girls who are best at

art. Miss Selby will order all the materials you need, some of the girls will make costumes, which you will design. They spare no expense here. Each year they have a stage built in the dining-room. You are going to be busy.''

Drina was rather overwhelmed.

"It sounds so big.''

"You can do it. I'll help you with the dancing, of course, though most of the ideas must come from you. Here they have you with your talents; let them see what it means. But keep the ballet *comme il faut*. Now her smile was really broad. "Modern, but not too modern. Remember it is a polite school for young girls.''

Drina laughed.

"It mustn't be like *The Rake's Progress*?''

"Most certainly not like that. Do you want poor Miss Selby to faint? And now you'll dance that solo again. There are points where I can help, though I'm no choreographer. Don't be afraid. You can do this, and it'll be good for you.''

Drina nodded. Already the ballet was growing in her mind and a deep excitement was stirring. To create something, instead of simply enduring ...

When the hour was over, and she ran to her cubicle to change, she stood by the window staring out at the lake, grey today in a faint mist of rain. *New York Rhapsody*! Her second ballet, and perhaps some day it might be danced at the Dominick.

The weeks no longer stretched dismally ahead. They were going to be packed with work.

BOOK TWO
Ballet in Company

1

"New York Rhapsody"

Until Signora Lerrani came again on the Friday Drina's mind was bursting with thoughts of the ballet. Within a few hours she had seen that there were going to be problems, for – counting Tamina and herself – there were only eleven girls who learned ballet, and there were no boys. Even if it had been possible to find male dancers in the town, Miss Selby would never agree. Therefore girls were going to have to dance the male parts, and how on earth was she going to fill the many roles that had taken shape in her mind?

Tamina, hearing all about it, said cheerfully:

"Only eleven learn ballet, but there are other girls in the school who have learned dancing of one kind and another. In any case, would all of them need to dance? The mothers and the down-and-outs and so on ... anyone could manage them."

"Yes, I suppose you're right, if they wouldn't mind. I *am* the youngest, and when they hear about it perhaps they'll think the whole thing really cheeky."

But Tamina thought there would be no chance of that.

"They know all about you. I think they'd enjoy it. They were very bored with that French play last Christmas, I believe, though I wasn't here until January. Fiora was here then and I've heard her say it was quite deadly. And as for the scenery – some of the girls are very good at art. I'm sure they'd love to work on a big backcloth."

There was no word from Miss Selby until Thursday afternoon, when Drina returned from a walk in the town. Then she was asked to go to the study.

Miss Selby was very gracious.

"Signora Lerrani tells me that you're going to compose a ballet for Christmas, and she seems quite certain that you know exactly what you want. You have my full permission to go ahead. It will make a very nice change for the parents and some of my own guests. But I hope you won't neglect your ordinary work."

"I won't, Miss Selby. Thank you." And Drina rushed away to snatch some time in the studio.

By Friday afternoon the general lay-out of the ballet was almost complete in her mind, though she was still troubled about numbers and the terrible lack of male dancers. She was working on the Stranger's solo, which was to be rather a swaggering dance, when Signora Lerrani arrived.

"That looks very exciting," said the ballet teacher.

Drina stopped and ran forward eagerly. Her face was bright and wholly alive.

"That's for the Stranger, the young man who steals the heroine for a little while. I mean him to be rather a show-off – kind of impressive and false at first. But then, for a time, he really does fall in love. But, Signora, I've thought of so many things that are difficult." And she poured out her problems.

Signora Lerrani listened with interest.

"Yes, I feel sure that some of the other girls would be willing to take the minor roles. And, of course, I thought of the problem of having no boys. You'll just have to do your best with what material you have here."

"Well, I thought of Helga for the Young Man, the one who keeps his girl in the end. She's fair and quite tall and you've sometimes said she's a good dancer. Then maybe Bianca for the Stranger; I have a feeling she could do it. Tamina's one of the best, isn't she? But she isn't tall enough to be a man, so I thought she could be the leading Puerto Rican girl. I suppose I'd better dance the Girl myself. Or will they think –?"

"Of course you must dance the main part. It will be taken for granted. And, yes, Helga, Bianca and Tamina, as you say."

"Then most of the others can be Puerto Ricans. Say four or five of them. I won't make it like *West Side Story*. Just a group to dance something very colourful and lively. Rather foreign. The children are the other really big problem. I just don't know where they're to come from and I did want them to do a ball dance."

Signora Lerrani was looking thoughtful.

"My sister teaches young children in the town. I think it possible that I could persuade Miss Selby to let you incorporate a few of them. Maybe you could go and teach them the dance and fit it into the ballet later. How would that be? Luckily there is plenty of time."

"It would be just fine, but would Miss Selby really let me?"

"She would probably insist on your being chaperoned, but no doubt it can be arranged."

Drina shrugged impatiently, but was too absorbed in her idea to argue.

"I'll try and get started on the backcloth and the costume designs this weekend. I'll take some paints home with me, and maybe I could borrow the New World record? There's a record-player at the villa. The costumes will be very simple really. It will be just a question of blending colours. The Puerto Rican girls can wear brilliant colours, and I thought probably white for me. Thank goodness there really is quite a lot of time. December 19th, we need it for. Then we break up the next day."

She arrived at the villa looking so much better and happier that both her grandparents were relieved. Mrs Chester was especially thankful, because she had been hearing a good deal to the effect that they should never have brought Drina to Switzerland. The weather, as it happened, was exceedingly wet, so Drina was able to avoid all distractions and settle down to the designing.

"All the same, I hope she isn't going to give all her time to this ballet," said Mrs Chester, sounding worried. "She has her school work to think of."

"She knows that. We can't interfere. It's what she needed," Mr Chester said. An hour later he went into the room where Drina was painting and found her flushed and untidy, with paint on her fingers and even her face. On the table before her were several postcard views of New York, which she had brought with her to Switzerland, and she was working on a large, striking painting. In the foreground were trees turning faintly gold and a hint of water, and behind rose a line of buildings, touched with blue as though in a heat haze. "Goodness, Drina! I didn't know you were such an artist!"

Drina indicated a scattering of abandoned attempts on the floor beside her.

"I've had a struggle. At first it wouldn't go right. That's Essex House, see. And Hampshire House. And the Plaza Hotel at the end, with its gables. And then far behind, the RCA Building and the Empire State."

"And those others at the very back that you've touched with silver paint to make them shine?"

"The Trade Towers. Of course you can't see them really – too far downtown. But I want to suggest them. I wish I could make it a bit more modernistic. But it's recognisable, isn't it?"

"It couldn't be anywhere but New York," he agreed gravely, much impressed. For the design was bold and confident.

"I wish there could be two scenes. I'd love to do a night backcloth ... all the buildings sparkling with lights. But I'll have to be content with one. I don't even know if we can have wings, but I'm going to do some. I shall make a proper little stage, all gummed together, the way Miss Whiteway does. I hope it looks all right when it's big. I've seen the Dominick workshops. I think I know what paint and materials we need, but I'm going to write to the Dominick and make sure."

"Well, don't tire yourself out."

"Oh, soon, I'm going to put on the New World and lie on my back and simply absorb it."

"I should think it's pretty well absorbed already. It's always been one of your favourites, hasn't it?"

"Yes, but now I have to see movement to it."

The news about *New York Rhapsody* was received with enthusiasm by most of the girls and Drina was besieged with questions. It seemed as though she would have no difficulty in finding any number to "walk on".

Life at the school was suddenly very different; there just didn't seem enough hours in the day to do all that she planned. The members of the staff viewed the change in her with amazement, for she now displayed a quiet confidence that made it hard to remember she was the youngest. She did not neglect her school work, either, but actually seemed to improve.

Only Madame Maréchel, who definitely did not like her, was wholly disapproving.

"To put so much in the hands of one young girl. It seems absurd to me. How do we know that she can do this thing? To dance is one thing, but making a whole ballet and giving orders ... in my opinion it's too much for her and not good for her, either."

"She knows exactly what she wants," said the art mistress, who had now seen the finished design for the backcloth and also the very detailed letter from the Dominick. "And her designs for the costumes are really very clever. So simple, but the colours unusual and good."

"And Signora Lerrani approves whole-heartedly," said Miss Green, who was most impressed by the change in the quiet and apparently difficult girl who had started the term.

Drina was too busy to mourn her lot as November ended and December came in with a few bright and almost warm days. The trees were bare now, and there was snow on the higher mountains, but sometimes it was possible to sit out of doors in sheltered corners of the garden.

She was not exactly resigned to her life at the school, but it was certainly very much better than she had thought at first. The growth of *New York Rhapsody* was exciting and sometimes astonished her. It was extraordinary that the whole thing had come out of her own mind and was taking concrete shape.

She still, however, thought a good deal about London and the Dominick and she read her letters with as much eagerness as ever. Rose had the part of Jane and was being understudied by a girl called Candy Smith in the class below. Most of the other main parts were being played by exactly the same cast as in Francaster, though instead of using local children in the *corps de ballet*, as they had done in the North, they were now using many of the younger juniors from the Dominick School.

I was terrified at first, Rose wrote, early in December, just after rehearsals had started in a London theatre, *but now I just love it. Only I wish I didn't keep on getting colds. At the moment I'm in danger of losing my voice, and that really frightens me.*

I was thrilled to hear all about New York Rhapsody. *Miss Volonaise asked me about you, and it seems that she's heard about your ballet, as you wrote to Mr Brown in the workshop. It sounds ten times more exciting than* Twentieth Century Serenade.

Drina wrote back:

I still envy you being Jane, but my ballet is certainly helping to make up for being here. We're starting to put it together now. Bianca is really amazingly good as the Stranger and Tamina is good, too. They're working terribly hard. I must confess that I didn't think that anyone here had it in them. They seemed such a lazy, frivolous lot when I came.

I went into the town to teach the kids and they are just sweet. I chose six and by incredibly good luck one of them is a little black girl called Sally. I knew it was wrong not to have some black people in the ballet, as Central Park is full of them, but I never thought to find one here.

Some of the girls who are best at art are painting the backcloth and it looks splendid, and we're all working on the costumes in the evening. I was worried about lighting at first, but I discovered that the rather cross old handyman, Enrico, is a wizard with electricity and he says he'll be able to do all I want.

I do hope your voice goes right. It must be very worrying.

But two days after she had posted the letter Drina had one from Ilonka, telling that Rose was away from school and rehearsals and said to be quite ill.

She kept on for too long, Ilonka wrote. *I do not think she has been very well for some time. And yesterday she collapsed at the rehearsal. She has a very bad throat and a temperature. Isn't it hard luck? But maybe she will be back soon.*

"Oh, poor Rose!" Drina said aloud, and her heart went out to her friend.

After a few days Rose herself wrote, very shakily, from bed.

Oh, Drina, I'm more miserable than I've ever been in my life. The doctor says I was an idiot to struggle on for so long and that I've nearly done serious damage to my throat. He won't hear of my going back into the play. He says I'm anaemic and run down as well, and need a rest.

Would you ever have believed that fate could be so unkind? I'm lying here and almost wishing I were dead. I wish I had a room to myself and a better view. I think often of Chalk Green and the lovely shapes of the hills and woods. Mum does her best; in fact, she's been wonderful, but nothing cheers me up for long. The cast of The Land of Christmas *sent me a huge basket of fruit, and – just fancy – Yvette Farthingale came to see me. You remember her? She plays the Midnight Witch, and after all she's a famous actress. That did cheer me for a while, and Mum was deeply impressed. They've seen Yvette on the television. She was in a Sunday night play quite recently.*

The only bright thing is that Dad won a prize on his Premium bonds. He says he would send me away somewhere for Christmas, but there seems nowhere to go.

Drina, haunted by the vision of Rose suffering in her overcrowded bedroom, with all her hopes in the dust, went home to the villa that weekend with a plan in her mind. She and her grandparents were going to Kandersteg for Christmas, to the hotel where they had stayed years before, and she could not see why Rose should not join her there.

"Granny, it's terrible for Rose. And her father won some money on Premium bonds, so he could pay her fare and perhaps something towards her hotel expenses. You know you said I've got a double room to myself at the hotel. They have so few single ones. Let me ask her. Oh, *please*, let me ask her!"

"But how would she get to Switzerland?" Mrs Chester asked.

"Oh, Granny. She's sixteen! She could manage and her family never fuss over her. She could book through Cook's or someone and then, if she got into any difficulty, she could ask one of the representatives. You know they're always about at the Channel ports and in Basle."

"I don't see why Rose shouldn't come," said Mr Chester, very firmly. "It *is* hard on the girl and Drina will enjoy Christmas much more with a friend her own age. Yes, you write and invite her, Drina."

"Oh, very well," said Mrs Chester. "You do as you please. You will anyway." But her tone was kind.

Drina immediately wrote to Rose and rushed out to post the letter. So, as well as her ballet, she now had thoughts of Christmas in the Alps with Rose to fill her mind. It would be wonderful to see her friend again, at least three months before she had expected to do so.

2
A Surprise for Drina

There were times when Drina had moments of panic over her ballet, for it was a far bigger thing than she had ever tackled before. But, for the most part, she enjoyed the last weeks of term.

The ballet provided exactly what was needed to counteract the usual restlessness of the weeks before Christmas, and the work it entailed brought Drina into contact with almost all the girls in one way and another. She found that she liked most of them very much, and even Francesca, who was a skilled needlewoman, seemed very interested. It was she who made Drina's simple white dress and did a great deal of the work on the more exotic clothes of the Puerto Rican girls.

There were sewing parties most evenings in the big sitting-rooms, often to the music from a radio or record-player.

The big backcloth was finished and the ballet itself was becoming a complete entity. Tamina was very good as the principal Puerto Rican girl and there were times when Drina and – if the truth were known – Signora Lerrani were sorry that she was unlikely to try and make ballet her career. Helga had worked amazingly hard at her role and was good, too, and Bianca adored being the Stranger.

"This ballet is everywhere," said Madame Maréchel gloomily. But she had not seen the dancing at all and had no real idea of what was going to emerge on the all-important date.

Just before Drina went home to the villa for the last weekend of term Rose wrote that she was coming to Kandersteg. She no longer seemed to want to die and was returning to the Dominick for the last week of term.

I must just accept that fate is sometimes unkind, she wrote. *And at least it isn't wholly unkind. I'm reading a lot about the Alps and dream every night of seeing snow-peaks. Mum is convinced that I shall get lost in darkest Europe, but I know I can manage. I've booked a couchette to Basle – doesn't that sound exciting? And I am looking forward to seeing you again.*

Drina went home in high spirits, and on the Saturday morning Signor and Signora Rionante, with Tamina, called for the Chesters and Drina in their huge car. They were borne swiftly to the pretty villa on the shores of Lake Maggiore, where they had lunch.

Drina was pleased to meet Tamina's little sister Carla, and was shown everything, including the boat that the family used on the lake in summer. Then she and Tamina walked into Locarno, which was so much smaller than Lugano, and Drina loved the Piazza Grande with its coloured buildings and market stalls. The monastery of Madonna del Sasso stood high above the town and Drina cried suddenly:

"Oh, let's climb up there! I feel full of energy."

"But it is very steep. There are many steps –"

"Never mind. Dancing hasn't by any means used up all my strength."

They climbed up and up under the bare trees. It was a perfect winter's day, with clear pale sunshine, and the

air was very still. And when they reached the high terraces at last, Drina leaned on the stone balustrade and gazed down at the bright roofs and at the vast, pale blue sweep of the lake. The higher mountains, touched with snow, made a distant frieze against a sky that was just a little bluer than the water and sounds travelled for a long way in the quiet air.

The lake went on for many miles into Italy, and Drina remembered how she had been to Stresa with her Italian grandmother and Igor, and how she had danced on Isola Bella.

"I love Switzerland," she said, after a long silence. "It's beautiful. But Italy means far more to me. I wish we could sail down the lake until we came there."

"The frontier is just beyond Brissago," said Tamina. "Perhaps in summer. It's lovely to do that on a hot day."

"But I shan't be here next summer. Goodness!" said Drina, with sudden realisation. "I've done nearly half of my exile. At first I thought it would never pass, but things got so much better as soon as you came."

Tamina sighed, her face suddenly grave.

"I shall miss you when you go away."

"But you'll be leaving yourself at Easter, and I don't forget my friends. You know they were saying at lunch that you must come and visit us in London, perhaps next summer."

"I've never seen England. I should like that."

"And you'd see the new Dominick and come to Covent Garden and the Dominick Theatre with me. Oh, we won't lose touch. How could we? And then I'm bound to go back to Milan. I could easily break my journey and stay with you."

"You'll be famous. A great dancer!"

"Oh, rubbish! Not for a long time, if ever. Though I

shall be a Senior Student next year – they've promised. In September, that is. Then I shall be walking on with the Dominick sometimes."

"But you've done so much more than walking on."

Drina frowned.

"I know. Rose once said that I wouldn't be keen on being in the *corps de ballet* after having solo roles and even starring parts. She's right, of course, but I must just forget all that. If they want me to be a fairy's attendant in *The Sleeping Beauty* or a rat or something like that, I shall have to do it and be glad. Even the *corps* won't come until later, when I'm actually in the Company."

They looked at the very ornate church and then hurried down the hillside again as the early dusk began to fall and lights sprang out in Locarno and the small villages around the lake. Later Signor Rionante drove them home and it had been a very happy day that Drina was to remember with pleasure.

So the last week of term came, with the great event due on the Thursday evening. The parents of many of the girls were travelling long distances and a number of hotel bookings had been made in the town.

On Monday morning men arrived to start putting up the quite ambitious stage in the dining-room and meals took place in two other smaller downstairs rooms.

The house was filled with the sound of sawing and hammering and the air of excitement grew and grew, so that not much actual schoolwork was done. Drina was now definitely nervous about the coming performance, sure that something would go wrong. It began to matter very much to her that Miss Selby should be pleased and impressed and it was known that the headmistress had invited a number of important people from the town.

The early weeks at the school had undermined Drina's confidence in herself, for it had been new and dreadful to be regarded as a rather unsatisfactory person, and the ballet seemed a chance to wipe out the earlier impression of her character.

Signora Lerrani, finding her pale and tense early on Wednesday afternoon, was reassuring.

"All will be well. You may take my word for it. The ballet is charming and everyone will love it. One day I feel sure it will be danced again in London, on a real stage. And now let us see how this dress rehearsal goes."

The children had arrived from the town and were laughing and talking amongst themselves. This was not their first visit to the school and the older girls loved them, especially the little dark-skinned Sally.

The stage was not, of course, as big as would have been desirable, but it was a very efficient job and the backcloth and wings looked far more effective than Drina had ever hoped. On the whole, too, everything went well, with everyone but the actual performers and helpers shut out.

"But tomorrow there'll be quite a large audience," Drina said, as they dispersed at last.

By Thursday morning all the seats were in place and glorious flowers began to arrive from a shop in Lugano. The buffet supper was to take place in the big drawing-room and was being provided by caterers. Certainly no expense had been spared.

A large number of the girls were taken to have their hair done in the morning and Drina was amongst them. She emerged with her shining black hair swinging in a perfect shape round her neck, and afterwards, since it was not at all cold, they walked back along the promenade. There were Christmas trees outside some of the hotels and plenty of visitors about, because many families chose to spend the holiday by the lake.

"The day after tomorrow we go to Kandersteg," said Drina.

"You'll ski, I suppose?" asked Bianca, who was very keen on winter sports and hoped to go to the Dolomites with her family after Christmas.

Drina shook her head regretfully.

"I'd love to, but I've decided it isn't worth the risk. It will cut me to the heart, but I shall get some skating, perhaps. I'm quite a good skater, but I've never tried ski-ing."

"It isn't so very risky," said Tamina. "Though a friend of mine broke her leg last year, and another injured her back."

Drina laughed.

"It sounds *quite* risky, the way you put it. I just daren't chance injuring myself: I know what a terrible fuss I'd make if I did. Dancing comes first. I shall content myself with skating and walking, if the weather's fine."

"This dancing!" said Antonia, who was with them. "You think of nothing else. To be in the Alps and not ski seems absurd to me."

"I know, but there it is," Drina said quietly. Just then she could not give many thoughts to the holiday in the Bernese Oberland. Only the ballet mattered and she had butterflies in her stomach whenever she thought about it.

The afternoon was spent putting last-minute touches to everything and then the girls were all sent to rest for an hour. Antonia slept, but Drina and Tamina lay writhing in excitement, wishing that the time would pass. Drina read again Jenny's last letter, that had arrived that morning.

Dear Drina, (Jenny wrote)
Best of luck with the ballet. I shall be thinking about you, and

I'm sure it will be a success. After all, anyway, what are these people to you? They probably don't know the first thing about real dancing.

It seems like a year since you went away. I really do rather hate my job, but I've gone all out to be efficient and they gave me a rise last week. I still see Timothy occasionally – he has a job in an insurance office, but still dreams of going in for forestry – but Robert and I meet every weekend now. There isn't much outdoor work on the farm now, of course, except for looking after the stock, but we did a wonderful job of whitewashing last weekend.

Did I ever tell you? The Hogdens now have Esmeralda. I still think of him as your cat. He was looking rather thin and the people who have taken over Uncle's farm didn't seem to mind him going. He is gloriously sleek again and always welcomes me.

Mark Playford wrote to me and says he hopes to see me in the holidays, when he's home from the Dominick. And I often see Joy Kelly, who also has an office job. She always asks after you, envying you because you are going to be – no, are – a real dancer.

Lucky you, going to the Alps. And lucky Rose. I wish my poor father could win some money somehow, but he doesn't even do the football pools.

Wish we could meet and have a good gossip.

And, in many ways, Drina wished it, too. Letters really did nothing to bridge the gap between herself and Jenny, though she could follow Jenny in imagination to Hogdens' farm and see her perched on a ladder, using a whitewash brush. But she could not quite imagine Jenny and Robert Hogden together. The big, red-haired young man who had once given them both a lift in his lorry. It seemed a very long time ago, in another life, and who would have thought then that he and Jenny would ever become such friends?

The bell rang and everyone began to stream down to tea, afterwards flying back upstairs to bath and change. The house rang with laughter and excited talk and all cubicle curtains were drawn back that day. Rules seemed to have been forgotten.

Francesca, in a beautiful dress from one of the great Rome fashion houses, even looked in to have a word with Drina, who was just ready in her Paris dress, with a blue and silver cape round her shoulders.

"Don't be nervous. Everything will go well."

But Drina was shiveringly nervous. What Jenny said wasn't true. Some of these girls' parents must see famous ballet companies in the cities where they lived. They might be all too ready to laugh at the efforts of a sixteen-year-old.

"I wish it were over, Francesca. I wish it came first, anyway."

The guests were expected to start arriving at six o'clock. They would wander about the house, see the art exhibitions and have drinks. Then would come the buffet supper and finally a few musical items, followed by the ballet.

The house was warm and bright, smelling of flowers, and Miss Selby walked about calmly, very dignified and even rather handsome in a black dress. Madame Maréchel looked like a Duchess, as Drina whispered to Tamina, and every other member of the staff had dressed up for the occasion.

Signora Lerrani arrived from the station in a taxi, and, following closely on her heels, the parents began to appear. The girls thronged the hall, flushed and bright-eyed, and Drina was fascinated to see the different parents. Helga's were there, both very tall and fair, and Lotti's dumpy, rather dowdy, but pleasant-faced mother. Francesca's mother was even more beautiful than her daughter, and her dress seemed to everyone fabulous.

Drina was just beginning to grow anxious in case something had happened to her grandparents when the door opened and in they came, both in evening dress.

Drina ran forward, then stopped abruptly, her face frozen into a look of total disbelief. For, behind the Chesters, was another figure: a tall woman who walked like a dancer.

"Miss Volonaise!" Drina gasped. "Oh, I'm dreaming! I *must* be dreaming. You can't be here!"

"Everyone is looking at you, Drina," said Mrs Chester, but she was smiling.

"But – but –"

Marianne Volonaise took her cold hand.

"I've been in Milan with Renée Randall. She's been appearing as guest artist at La Scala. I had some arrangements to make with the people there, to do with our next tour in the spring, so I thought I could kill several birds at once. Your grandparents very kindly asked me to spend the night at the villa."

The hall had stopped whirling round, but Drina was still dazed with shock.

"But – but, Miss Volonaise, *you* can't see my ballet! It's just a school thing ... I didn't mean ... I didn't think –"

"Of course I can see it," said Marianne Volonaise calmly. "That's why I've come."

3

The Performance

Drina led them to take off their outdoor clothes, trying desperately to gather her wits together. That one of the Directors of the Dominick had cared enough to come and see *her* seemed quite unbelievable, even if Marianne Volonaise did know about Elizabeth Ivory and had been her friend.

Drina had thought herself exiled far from Red Lion Square, but the Dominick had come to her, in Switzerland. It was wonderful, but it was also terrifying. Nervous before, she now felt that she would probably die before the ballet ever took the stage.

Her grandfather said in a low voice, as they walked towards the drawing-room:

"She seemed most anxious to come. She said she had to see your second ballet. I don't think there's any need to be scared."

"*Scared*! I'm blue with fright already. But, oh! I am so glad to see her! I'm so honoured –"

"She's fond of you and interested in you, too. She doesn't mean to let you go."

Drina did the honours as best she could, and was quite unaware of the charming dignity with which she introduced them to people and led them about the school. Tamina pretty in pale green, realised more than anyone the importance of what had happened to Drina. *She* knew that the directors of ballet schools did not readily put themselves out to see the efforts of a young student.

Signora Lerrani, who had met Miss Volonaise only the previous day in Milan, had been in the secret and was bracing about Drina's nerves.

"Don't be silly, my dear. The ballet's good." But in her heart she was puzzled – not knowing about Elizabeth Ivory and the high hopes felt about her daughter – to understand just why Marianne Volonaise had come to Lugano.

"But still,' she said to herself, "the girl is one of their star pupils and a professional also."

Now everyone had arrived and it was time for supper. Drina, convinced that she could eat nothing, found herself very neatly and quietly possessed by Miss Volonaise and held in a corner.

"Eat something, Drina. It will have time to go down before you're ready to dance. And stop looking like that. I shan't be too critical. I'm sure there must have been endless difficulties. This seems a delightful place, but it's not the place for you. Have you been very unhappy? Rose seems to think that you have. And you're certainly thinner."

"I *hated* it at first, and I'm not looking forward to next term, when there'll be nothing so exciting as *New York Rhapsody*. I – I didn't behave well. I hated all the silly rules ... not being able to go out alone ... all that. People didn't approve of me. But the last few weeks have been much better. And my Italian is very fluent now. I'm glad of that. But please tell me. How is Rose?"

Marianne Volonaise frowned.

"Poor Rose! She was cut to the heart to lose Jane. It was most unfortunate and we all felt for her. She was good in the part, though not as good as you. You look so much younger, for one thing. The other girl, Candy, will be all right. You remember her, don't you? We gave her permission to be in pantomime last year and she had quite a leading part. Rose has got over it and seems better, but she's far too pale. Her slight delicacy worries us all. Well, it isn't exactly delicacy, though she has a return of the anaemia that worried us so much years ago. That was why she was sent to Chalk Green, of course, and she was much better for a long time. Anyway, she'll be fine after her holiday in the Alps. She says something is sure to happen to stop her going. I spoke to her just before I left for Milan."

"Oh, she'll come. She'll be leaving London on Sunday and I'll meet her in Kandersteg on Monday."

"It's what she needs. I've been telling your grandparents."

While they had been talking Drina had managed to eat something, but, all the same, Monday in the Alps still seemed a long way off. She glanced at her watch and said:

"I ought to be going to change now. I'm helping the others to make up. Of course there's some music before the ballet. Oh, I do wish it were over!"

"Rubbish! You'll enjoy it. And next year who knows? It may find a place in the Dominick matinée programme."

Drina, with a word to her grandparents, went off to tell her cast that it was time to get ready. Tamina went pale; she was nervous, too. And Helga vowed that she was suffering agonies of stage fright.

But Drina, once she was wearing the simple dress, with its soft folds, and was made up, felt steadier. Her hand did not shake at all as she applied make up to some of the others, tried to quiet the excited small

children and did a hundred and one other things.
Luckily the stage had been built just where there were
two doors immediately behind the wings, each leading
into a corridor, and the cast was assembling in the office
and another small room near by. One of the girls had
volunteered to be "call boy" and had done an efficient
job at the dress rehearsal, so there should be no
muddles. The strains of someone's cello solo came to
them as they all waited nervously.

Signora Lerrani, who, like Drina, had seemed to be in
a dozen places at once, came to say reassuringly:

"Don't worry. Everything will be all right. Enrico is
ready with the lights, and I will see to the music."

Out in the audience Marianne Volonaise sat next to
the Chesters. In her hand was a copy of the programme
and she sat looking down at it.

New York Rhapsody
Music by Dvorak, Choreography by Drina Adams
Book, Set and Costumes by Drina Adams
Ballet Mistress Signora Lerrani

Then there were the names of the dancers and the rest
of the cast, followed by a resumé of the story:

*The scene is Central Park, in New York City, on an autumn
afternoon. The park is crowded with people: mothers wheel
prams ... down-and-outs sleep in the sun ... girls pass on
their way to roller skate or play tennis ... children play with
a ball.*

*The Stranger is remote, apart; a compelling figure, at first
only interested in himself. But then he sees the Girl and the
Young Man, who seem absorbed in each other, and he wishes
to attract the Girl. He succeeds, in spite of the Young Man's*

efforts to keep her, and the Stranger and the Girl experience a brief rhapsody, she gradually believing in him and experiencing a happiness she had never known possible.

But the Young Man will not let her go and he and the Stranger compete for her. The Stranger, who perhaps never really believed in the rhapsody himself, finally goes and the Girl is bereft. Yet, as night comes, she turns again to her old love, though things will never be the same for her. She has rejected the Stranger, who is now more alone than ever, and she is not now sure what life holds for her.

Drina Adams! Only just sixteen and yet tackling such a theme. Marianne Volonaise thought back to the child who had come to the Dominick nearly four years before – a little black-haired thing who had at first seemed no more remarkable than all the other students of her year. Yet, before a year had passed, that same child had been taking the leading part in a West End play and displaying a surprising strength of character when the play was a rather splendid failure and she had to return to the hard work of every day.

Drina had shown strength of character all through, thought the woman who had known Elizabeth Ivory, had, in fact, watched red-haired Betsy Chester's fight towards greatness. Drina had personality and talent and possibly she would turn into as fine a dancer as her mother. It was too early to tell, but the signs were there. And, not content with this, the girl was turning towards choreography. The one little ballet she had so far done had been simple enough; this second one sounded remarkably ambitious. It seemed unlikely that she could pull it off, with the difficulties of an all-female cast, a small stage and such music. But – well, one would see.

Sitting in that warm, crowded room in a finishing-school in Lugano, Marianne Volonaise found herself as tense and keyed up as though this were some important first night in a great theatre.

And then the short concert was over; the stage was bare, brilliantly lighted. The backcloth was extraordinarily effective. Sets and costumes, too!

"She's been too ambitious," murmured Mrs Chester uneasily.

It seemed extremely likely.

Then the wonderful music of the New World Symphony filled the big room and the stage was bare no longer. There they all were, the mothers pushing their prams, the down-and-outs, the Puerto Ricans – dancing briefly – the children, darting and laughing, a little black girl carrying a huge red ball. And then the Stranger entered.

Bianca was a striking-looking girl, dark and vivid. With her short hair and slim figure she made a more than passable young man, wearing a soft blue shirt and dark trousers. Her carriage was always good and now she leaped in, conveying clearly that the Stranger did not belong to any group; that he did not, perhaps, even belong to this city. Her *grandes jetés* had been endlessly coached by Signora Lerrani, and Bianca had worked as never before.

Then the Girl and the Young Man were there, the Girl in her soft white dress, the tall, fair youth obviously devoted to her, sure that she was his.

But the Stranger had noticed the Girl and something had happened to him. He no longer wished to be remote and apart. As the music grew louder and more violent he began to attract the Girl away from her lover.

The Girl's long solo came at the beginning of the second movement and now the audience was very still. For there was something about the black-haired, white-clad figure that was far removed from an amateur performance at the end of term. Marianne Volonaise sat up straighter and knew the exact moment when Drina forgot to be nervous and lost herself in the dance. "Dear heaven! And we let her go," she said to herself. "Only for a while, but we ought to have done more to keep her. And yet she's learned something here, surely? She's bound to learn; she's the kind that will always grow."

But the girl on the stage was not Drina Adams; she was a young girl in New York City, bewildered by the thing that was happening to her ... awakening to a new experience. Yet, Drina Adams herself had been in Manhattan and she could see, as she danced, the buildings that lay around the park. Most clearly she could see the apartment building on Central Park West where Grant Rossiter lived. That had been a New York rhapsody indeed; those hot autumn days of magic and awakening love.

Then the Stranger was dancing, too, as the music grew louder and more compelling, and this was the real weakness of the ballet, Drina knew. Her *pas de deux* with the Stranger and her later one with the Young Man. Aware of the difficulties, she had not tried to compose a classical *pas de deux*. Bianca could not manage lifts, though she had proved herself, amazingly, a strong partner.

The Puerto Ricans broke into the *pas de deux* at last and Drina had enjoyed planning their *pas de six*, with a short solo for Tamina. She stood with the Stranger's arm about her, occasionally looking up at him.

Then the children did their dance, tossing the great scarlet ball, the little black girl tumbling and clowning. She had talent already.

But the Young Man was not beaten; he was going to keep his girl. And gradually one felt the spell between

the Girl and the Stranger breaking. The Stranger did a brief solo and shrugged and turned away, walking – an arrogant yet curiously sad figure – out of the park.

The lights began to dim as the Girl and the Young Man danced. Evening was coming ... everyone was going home. Once more the girls with their roller skates and tennis rackets passed, pausing to do a few dancing steps. The mothers, too, went their way and even the down-and-outs rose and soon wandered off.

And now the Girl and the Young Man were alone, looking at each other, trying to understand what had happened and wondering if they still had each other. They danced on for a moment, then stood in a single spotlight, which also made the further buildings shine. The girls who had done the backcloth had created a wonderful illusion with special paint.

The music came to an end and there was quite a long silence before the applause began.

Everyone came on stage to take a bow and then Drina had to go forward alone. She felt limp and tired now and a good deal frightened. The audience had liked the ballet, but had Miss Volonaise? Anyway, it was over.

Miss Selby then made a speech, in which she thanked everyone for providing such an interesting and unusual entertainment.

"I know very little about ballet," she said, smiling charmingly. "And I assure you all that this is the first time I have seen *New York Rhapsody*. I confess myself quite surprised. I had no idea that we possessed so much talent. I would especially like to thank Signora Lerrani and Drina Adams for all their hard work, and I know you would like to join me."

The applause was warm and prolonged.

The dancers then mingled with the audience without troubling to change or remove their make up, and

Drina, shrinking a little, could no longer put off facing Marianne Volonaise, who was with the Chesters and Signora Lerrani.

Mrs Chester was saying very little. She had been moved and very much startled by this ballet that had grown out of Drina's imagination. Imperfect it may have been, but it was not the work of a child. There had been moments of strange maturity.

"It was very nice, Drina," she said, in her undemonstrative way. "I'm sure everyone enjoyed it."

"*I* certainly did," said Mr Chester, who was not quite so surprised, for he had long suspected that Drina had her secret emotional life.

Marianne Volonaise looked at Drina gravely, but with a hint of a smile in her eyes. She signalled her to move a little to one side.

"Don't look so scared. *I* enjoyed it, too. The Dominick will want it some day, and of course it will be far, far better with a mixed cast. You can then develop the male dancing. But it was a very brave try by those girls, particularly Bianca. She showed much promise."

"Oh, Miss Volonaise, I'm so glad you didn't think it quite awful!"

"I thought the whole was most impressive. And at times you showed a quite remarkable appreciation and understanding of the music. Quite frankly, I don't know how you did it."

"Signora Lerrani helped a lot."

"And the Girl's solo would not need altering at all. I thought that was a little bit of nearly perfect dancing. I was proud of you then."

Drina stared at her wordlessly, for it was unbelievably high praise. Miss Volonaise laughed and suddenly kissed her on the cheek.

"People are starting to leave. I believe that the

Rionantes are giving us a lift back to the Villa Mimosa. You'll be home tomorrow, and mind you have a wonderful Christmas with Rose."

Still dazed, Drina said goodbye, but it was some time before everyone got to bed. Things had to be tidied up a little and then the whole affair talked over while the girls fortified themselves with the remainder of the supper.

Drina and Tamina talked for another half-hour when they were in bed, and Antonia joined in occasionally. She was pleased that Drina had had such a success, but now she felt more definitely than ever that she and her cousin had little in common. Perhaps, before next term, she would try tactfully to see if she could sleep in another room.

Drina, settling down to sleep at last, thought sadly:

"I've lost Antonia and it's a pity. But everything else is far better than I ever expected. I haven't disgraced myself here, after all. I think Miss Selby really was pleased.'

4
To the Alps

The next morning all was bustle and excitement and the girls with the longest journeys began to depart early. Drina agreed willingly enough to staying with Tamina to help with the clearing up, and finally the backcloth was down, the costumes were carefully stored for some future occasion when they might come in useful, and the last of their own packing was done.

Mr Chester came for Drina in a taxi, and, with all the luggage, she sped through the town, back to the Villa Mimosa. By then Miss Volonaise had left for England.

"I shouldn't unpack your trunk," said Mrs Chester. "Just leave most of the things in it and pack what you think you'll need in Kandersteg in your largest suitcase. Remember it's going to be snowy there. I believe they've had more snow than usual this December. Sometimes there's very little as low as four thousand feet until well into January."

"But, Granny, I've got time to unpack properly."

"Do as I say," said Mrs Chester, so sharply that Drina looked startled. But her grandmother went on, more gently: "I don't think you've noticed that great pile of Christmas post that's waiting for you."

Drina hadn't and she immediately rushed across to the side table and began to go through the letters and parcels, forgetting the question of unpacking. There seemed to be presents and cards from most of her friends in England, and there were two American parcels. One was from Yolande and the other – Drina's heart leaped – was from Grant.

Hastily she carried them all into the privacy of her bedroom and dropped all but Grant's small package on the bed. Last year she had almost prayed that Grant would remember her; this year she had scarcely had time to think about it. Her fingers fumbled with the knots and finally a flat box tied up with coloured ribbon was revealed. In it was a very pretty silver and blue necklace and a card that said: "Wear this sometimes when you go to the theatre. And I hope you and your grandparents have a very happy Christmas. Yours ever, Grant."

Drina was so happy at that moment that she hardly knew what to do with herself. Grant still remembered her; he had sent this pretty personal thing. He seemed suddenly very near; she almost heard his gently drawling voice.

The necklace had to be displayed amongst all the other presents, though Grant's card was safely tucked away in Drina's bag. Mrs Chester looked at the necklace with a faintly disapproving expression on her face.

"Now why should Grant Rossiter send you that? He scarcely knows you. That is, I should have thought he would have forgotten you long ago, being so much older."

Mr Chester said nothing, beyond admiring the present.

Drina had already managed to do a good deal of her Christmas shopping at weekends, and presents and cards had already gone off to England and America. This year she had, after some thought and a few doubts, sent Grant a present – a book of beautiful Swiss photographs – but he would not have received it when he posted his parcel to her. So they had both been thinking of each other.

But there were still things to buy and she spent a delightful couple of hours wandering round the Lugano shops. For her grandmother she chose a scarf and gloves, for her grandfather a quite expensive wallet – his old one was very shabby – and some pretty slippers for Lucia. She had nothing for Rose yet and this seemed the greatest problem. She wanted to buy something very nice and she finally decided on a rose-coloured sweater. They did not usually buy each other expensive presents, but Rose needed cheering up, if she wasn't cheered already by the time she had travelled up that exciting railway line to Kandersteg.

"Are you taking some shoes and a dress that you can dance in?" asked Mrs Chester that evening. "I rather feel that Frau Braun may want you to dance at Christmas. Remember how you danced when we stayed there before? She reminded me in a letter. It seems she's never forgotten 'the little dancer'."

"Oh, of course I will, Granny, if she asks me. I'd already thought of it and warned Rose to bring her ballet shoes."

Saturday dawned bright and amazingly warm and it seemed silly, as they drove to the station, to be wearing so many clothes, even thick boots.

"I feel like an arctic expedition!" grumbled Drina, flinging off her coat as soon as they were settled in the train. "Phew!"

"You'll need everything before the day is over."

It was a long and awkward journey to Kandersteg. North of the Alps the snow was deep in most places and the sky was grey, promising more snow. It was bitterly cold on the platform at Spiez and Drina suddenly began to have a feeling of adventure. Above them were the great mountains of the Bernese Oberland and soon they would go speeding upwards, spiralling along the precipice into that high world.

And when they were in the last train, which had come from Germany and was going on to Milan by the Lötschberg route, she stood in the corridor, trying to keep the steaming panes clear. The River Kander came roaring down in a grey-green torrent and the wooden chalets of the Oberland were a great change from the little stone houses and villas of the Ticino. The long, overhanging roofs were covered with snow, and the fir-trees, white-tipped, made the scene look exactly like a Christmas card.

Up and up they went, the electric engine dashing in and out of tunnels, and Drina looked down unflinchingly into the valley now far below. It was growing dark, but occasionally she caught glimpses of dazzlingly white peaks above. The Doldenhorn, perhaps.

Then they swept up into the Kander Valley as snow began to fall in big, fluffy flakes, partly obscuring the stark limestone precipices that edged the valley on one side. But Drina cried out when she looked the other way and spied the wonderful winged peaks of the Blümlisalp, seen for a moment through the snow.

"Oh, it's marvellous to be back!"

Her memories of Kandersteg were all summer ones; of flower-filled meadows and sunlight on high ice and snow. She still clearly remembered the day she had climbed to the edge of the Kander glacier, wearing a big red sunhat, and it had been hot all the way so that they had stopped often to pick wild strawberries.

It was very different now in the snowy dusk. The

sound of sleigh-bells rang out in the long village street and lights were already shining brightly. A Swiss band was playing, as it had done before in that long ago August, but this time the sound of a Christmas carol filled the air, *See Amid the Winter Snow*.

It was not far to their hotel, so they walked, leaving the luggage to follow, and Mrs Chester grew a little fretful because Drina would keep on stopping to look into the bright shop windows.

"We've had a long day and the snow is getting worse. Do hurry up, please, Drina."

"But it's another world, Granny. I can't believe that we haven't come to another country."

People in ski-ing clothes passed them in laughing groups and there was the constant jingle of skates as they were swung in warmly gloved hands. Drina's thick boots were very welcome now and the snowflakes tickled her cheeks coldly. She thought of Earls Court and wondered what Rose would make of this high mountain village. It was going to be wonderful to watch her friend's reactions and to explore with her.

The hotel was on the edge of the meadows, on the way to the Sesselbahn. The porch was strung with coloured lights and there was a Christmas tree on the veranda. The eaves were hung with icicles and the whole made a very pretty picture in the falling snow.

As the Chesters and Drina approached the steps a young man and a girl walking from the opposite direction came almost face to face with them. He was about seventeen, tall and rather dashing in a black and red ski-suit. The girl, who was very like him, also wore black and red, and skates dangled from their hands. They were laughing and talking together, but the boy's eyes suddenly met Drina's. He grinned and Drina smiled back.

In the warm entrance hall there were more young people and she thought cheerfully that it looked like being a merry Christmas. But there was not much time for thought just then, because Frau Braun came out of the office and gave them a warm welcome. Somehow they were drawn into the office where weak tea and little cakes were quickly produced, while the happenings of the years were detailed on either side.

Frau Braun expressed herself as amazed that Drina still looked so young.

"Sixteen! But one would never believe it, even with the lipstick." Drina had absolutely refused to face the holiday world without some make up. "But so pretty, and very travelled now, I believe."

"I speak German fairly well now, too," Drina told her.

"Then we will speak it sometimes, just to keep you in practice. But you'll find that most of us speak the valley dialect more often than we use High German. And you will dance for us? On Christmas Eve we will have a concert. But are you too grand now?"

"Oh, no, I'll dance. And so will my friend Rose, I expect." Drina had brought a record of *Twentieth Century Serenade* with her and had planned that they would do her own little ballet.

By the time they emerged from the office all the luggage had arrived and they were conducted upstairs, the Chesters to a large room on the first floor and Drina to one two floors higher, under the roof. It had two beds, both with billowing duvets. The floor was so brightly polished that it was rather a danger and Drina treated it with caution. The shutters were closed and the curtains drawn, and the room was very warm.

She longed to know which way the window faced, and if she and Rose would have a view of the mountains, but it was already dark and she would have to wait patiently until morning.

She flung off her coat and flopped on to the nearest bed, and the soft down immediately billowed up around her. Now she realised that she was very tired and it was almost too much trouble to unpack. She sat there for quite a long time, looking back at the term, deeply glad that there would be a break of more than three weeks before she need return. In spite of the success of her ballet she could not look forward with any pleasure to three more months of Madame Maréchel, unnecessary rules and a dreadful lack of personal freedom.

She came to herself with a start. It was silly to worry about the future when there were so many immediate delights in store. She unlocked her big case and began to fling her possessions right and left in search of a dress for the evening. It was all going to be fun.

The boy and girl she had seen by the steps were English twins, David and Deborah Collis. They were in Kandersteg with their parents, but seemed to see little of them. They did not even sit with them, but shared a table with a young Scottish boy and his sister.

Drina knew them all by the time the evening was half-over, and the younger guests were dancing in a room off the dining-room. Deborah and the Scottish boy, Ian, seemed very friendly and danced together, but Mary MacLaren seemed to prefer a tall, fair German boy to David. This apparently suited David, who made a beeline for Drina.

He was not much of a dancer, and, by Drina's standards, seemed very young for his age, but he was quite an amusing companion and the company of any boy seemed reasonably exciting after three months in the Lugano "nunnery".

David was a keen skater and a beginner at ski-ing. He

appeared to be the kind who did not like to do anything badly and was extremely rueful over his ski-ing mishaps. But he was amazed to hear that Drina was not going to try.

"But why on earth not? Everyone does. Everyone who isn't actually infirm, that is. Don't say your grandparents are against it, because, if so, I'll get my mother to have a tactful word with them."

"They're not against it. I could learn to ski if I wanted to. I *do* want to, but I've decided against it myself. I'm a dancer and I can't risk any broken bones."

"A dancer?" He promptly missed a step and fell painfully over Drina's small feet.

"A ballet student," she said modestly.

"You mean you learn all that business of dancing on your toes? No wonder you look like you do." He blushed and missed another step. "Good heavens! Where will you dance? At Covent Garden?"

"No, at the Dominick Theatre, I hope," she said, and did not enlarge on her past achievements.

"Still, I don't suppose you'd break anything. Of course people do, but it needn't happen. But perhaps you haven't brought the right clothes? You could easily buy them."

"Oh, I've the clothes," she said, for, with skating and snowy walking in mind, she had bought attractive dark green trousers and anorak in Lugano some weeks before. "I'll skate, that's all. But I have to buy or hire some skates. Actually, there's another reason. I've a friend joining me on Monday and I don't think she'd want to ski." For, quite apart from the possibility of broken bones, Rose would not have the money for ski-ing lessons, or the clothes, either.

Drina went to bed fairly early and slept heavily.

Awaking at nearly nine o'clock, she leaped out of bed and ran to the window, skidding on the polished floor. Flinging the shutters back, she gasped at the cold and the brilliant light. She hastily put on slippers and a warm dressing-gown and leaned out over the frozen sill, drinking in the wonderful view of the Blümlisalp, every peak harshly white against a sky of palest blue. The white meadows stretched away towards the lines of dark firs, and then the mountains rose up and up, unbelievably.

Men were sweeping the snow off the ice in a meadow near by, probably the hotel skating rink, and a horse-drawn sleigh went down the lane with a jingle of bells. But the intense cold drove her to shut the window and to turn up the heating, and she sang while she dressed.

It was an exhilarating day, for the bright air made her feel wholly alive. The skiers had gone off early, taking the Sesselbahn up to the higher slopes, but David stayed to skate with Drina and in the afternoon they were joined by some young new arrivals. As the early dusk fell a party of them wandered up the village street, which was very long indeed, and Drina found that she remembered it all very well, even some of the shops.

The shape of the Gellihorn was etched against the last of the daylight and the stars began to shine brilliantly. Lugano seemed very, very far away and all the troubles and stresses and final successes of the term. She only needed Rose to complete her present happiness and her friend would arrive the next morning at twelve o'clock.

5

Dancing for Joy

Drina was on the station platform by a quarter to twelve, too excited to keep still. There had been fresh snow in the night and it crunched under her boots as she walked restlessly up and down.

The sky was clear now, a dazzling, unlikely blue, and the mountains hadn't a cloud on them. The sight of the wonderful peaks could still almost stop her heart and she wondered again how the girl from Earls Court would feel in this unreal brilliance of winter snow.

The sun was almost hot on her shoulders and the snow underfoot was starting to melt. She heard the distant roar of a train, but it was coming the other way, bursting out of the great tunnel in the mountains that was the way to the Rhone Valley and Italy. She was so intent at staring at the long train that drew up at the opposite platform that she did not hear Rose's train coming until the electric engine was almost level with her. The coaches passed her one by one, labelled "Brig, Milano", and her heart began to beat wildly, for now she feared that her friend had not come.

Then she saw a wildly waving hand and began to run towards the back of the train, reaching Rose as she began to climb down the steep steps.

"Oh, Rose! Rose! I was suddenly so afraid that you

wouldn't be on it. Is that your case? Oh, the porter will bring it up to the hotel." And she spoke a few words of German to the man while Rose stood dazedly on the platform. She was wearing her Dominick uniform and what seemed to be new boots and thick gloves.

"Drina, I *must* be dreaming! It can't any of it be real. All the way after Thun I kept on pinching myself. Drina, I saw the Eiger, the Mönch and the Jungfrau and I nearly died at the beauty of them. I didn't know ... I never imagined ... Coming up from Spiez there was the river and the precipice and now *this*." And Rose walked to where she could see the Blümlisalp and stood in everyone's way, while Drina laughed a little shakily and tried to take her friend's arm.

"You look completely moonstruck. Oh, Rose, I *am* glad to see you! I've missed you so much."

"Moonstruck! I'm drunk and beaten and totally unbelieving. I'm glad now that I didn't die. And I'm glad to see you. You look fantastic in those clothes."

"Well, let's start walking. You nearly got that trunk on your head."

"It's just too much for me," said Rose, obeying. "You're used to it, but just let me go on gasping for a little longer."

"I'm not very used to it. Lugano is nothing like this."

"It's nothing like Earls Court, either, ducks." And Rose continued to exclaim as they walked down the road from the station towards the main village street. "Oh, the chalets! I love the gabled roofs. And the sound of bells and music, and the clean snow. But most of all the mountains! You must tell me all the names," she went on, standing on the bridge and staring down at the foaming Kander. "Oh, Drina, I haven't been so happy since we were in Paris. Well, except when I thought I was going to play Jane." Her face clouded.

"That was terribly hard luck. Miss Volonaise came to Lugano, you know, to see my ballet, and she told me how sorry everyone was."

Rose's face brighened again.

"She telephoned me before I left home yesterday. Fancy! So friendly and chatty. Told me about your ballet and how good it was, and said she hoped I'd have a good time with you here. Wasn't that absolutely wonderful of her? You'd think they'd all be utterly sick with me for letting them down. I went to the first night of *The Land of Christmas*, you know. It opened on Friday. Miss V. was there, but I didn't speak to her then. Flew back just in time. Candy Smith was really good, but I felt as jealous as anything. It was pretty grim."

"I suppose she'll get it next year, if they decide to do the play every Christmas," Drina said sadly.

"More than likely. You'll really be too old then and so shall I. Besides, we'll have other fish to fry, if we're Senior Students. Life will be real and earnest."

Drina agreed and they walked on, pausing often for Rose to do more exclaiming. When they neared the hotel she insisted on standing in the middle of a snowy meadow and having the names of all the peaks explained to her.

"I shan't forget. That tooth is the Birre, and that odd curved one at the end of the valley the Gellihorn. And the others are the Blümlisalp, the Doldenhorn and the Fisistock. Oh, and the Löhner over there, behind the cliffs and the fir woods. The Blümlisalp is quite perfect. I wish we could get nearer."

"Oh, we can. We can go up in the Sesselbahn and walk through the woods to the Oeschinensee. Not today, though, as it gets dark early and you'll want a rest after lunch. Then there's the concert tomorrow. We ought to practise if we're to do my ballet. Do you mind?

Did you bring your shoes and a suitable dress?"

"I don't mind and yes, I brought them. I'm not tired, either. I could never be tired here. Is *that* the hotel? What a picture! And everyone skating in the meadow. Are they fun?"

Drina nodded.

"Lots of young people. You must meet them soon. I've rather got stuck with David Collis. He's just a kid – seventeen and a bit of a show-off. But quite fun. You can't know how wonderful it is to be free and with boys again. I feel like doing something crazy."

Rose grinned.

"Not with your granny around! Think of her tender susceptibilities. Besides, after all that *comme il faut* you ought to be a little lady."

"I'm sick of *comme il faut*! I need something a great deal more down to earth. I want to have fun. Granny's being very mild; rather subdued, in fact. I'm a bit puzzled."

"Well, she got her way, didn't she? She hasn't got much to moan about as far as you're concerned."

"I suppose not. I just dread next term. Now I'm away from the place I see how much it oppressed me, in spite of *New York Rhapsody*, and that was good experience."

"Well, don't think of it. We're here and it's Christmas. What could be better than that?"

Rose was, of course, right, and they had a wonderful time. Rose was immediately accepted into the group and a young Frenchman, who had arrived the previous day, seemed very attracted to her. Rose took it calmly; she was used to Igor.

The concert took place after dinner on Christmas Eve and was a very cheerful, amateur affair for the most part. David recited some humorous verses, Deborah sang pop songs with a good deal of noise and fervour –

Mrs Chester frowned over this item, finding it vulgar – a party of Swiss guests yodelled, someone else played the piano. Drina's little ballet, *Twentieth Century Serenade*, came last and she thoroughly enjoyed it. It was good to dance without any thought of critics and without a sense of strain.

Few people in that quite large audience had any knowledge of ballet, but they could see that it was pretty and charming and far above the other items on the programme.

Soon afterwards David rushed up to Drina.

"Hey! That Mrs Gordon – the rather stuffy, smart one who doesn't have much to do with anyone – says you're quite famous, and that she saw you as Margaret in a West End production of *Dear Brutus*. It isn't true, is it?" His flushed face looked comically amazed and almost dismayed.

Drina laughed, amused by his tone.

"I was Margaret. I'm not famous though."

"But she says you're the bright hope of the Dominick Ballet Company. She knows someone who's something to do with Covent Garden and she hears all the ballet gossip. She says you danced with the Dominick at the Edinburgh Festival and in Paris. You said you were just a ballet student." His voice was accusing.

"I *am* a ballet student. The other things were just incidents. Rose danced in Edinburgh and Paris, too, come to that."

David, flummoxed, was noticeably subdued for the rest of the evening.

It snowed heavily on Christmas Day, but there was plenty to do within the hotel, apart from eating, which, as Rose remarked, took up a lot of time. The food seemed to her unbelievably wonderful and she moaned that she would go home pounds heavier. Drina wore

Grant's necklace in the evening and once found herself looking back to the previous Christmas in Francaster, when she had felt so sad, walking round the town walls in the cold grey light. She thought of Grant in New York, too, in the apartment on Central Park West, and wondered what he was doing. But mostly she was too busy to think at all.

Then followed a series of lovely days. Though it snowed most nights, the sun shone during the daylight hours and she and Rose were out nearly all the time. Rose was quite a good skater and they enjoyed themselves on the flooded, frozen meadow. They often went up in the Sesselbahn to watch the skiers or to walk through the meadows and woods to the lake under the sheer slopes of the Blümlisalp, and Rose was enchanted with everything. She grew pink-cheeked and even prettier than usual and was very popular.

One day the Chesters, Drina and Rose went to Berne and Drina told Rose the dreadful story of the weekend there with Madame Maréchel. It was easy to laugh now that she was free, but sometimes the thought of the coming term hung over her like a cloud.

Another day, after much teasing and arguing on Drina's part, she and Rose were actually allowed to go to Italy alone. It was perfectly possible to go to Milan and back in a day, having several hours there, and, though Mrs Chester was against the project, Drina won in the end, following a telephone call to her Italian grandmother, who had been away for Christmas, but was now back at the flat.

Rose was nearly beside herself with excitement as they sped along the precipice above the Rhone Valley just as the sun rose behind the eastern peaks, for to her it was the greatest of miracles to be going to Italy. Drina conducted the whole affair with the calm of an experienced traveller and they were met by Signora Adamo at the Stazione Centrale and given lunch at a huge hotel. Afterwards Rose saw the Cathedral and the Piazza del Duomo, the outside of La Scala and a great many other things, and her respect for Drina was greatly increased because she seemed to belong in the alien land.

"But I *am* half-Italian," Drina protested, laughing, as they sped back along the shores of Lake Maggiore in the last of the daylight. Mrs Chester had insisted that they must return very early.

"I know, of course, but I never realised what it meant. It all seemed so *foreign* to me, much more so than Switzerland or Paris." And then Rose stood in the corridor, in silence, watching the lights springing out on the romantic Borromean Islands.

The train passed through the great Simplon Tunnel and then, after climbing the vast slopes again, through the Lötschberg Tunnel, and they were back in the snowy Kander Valley under the bright winter stars.

It had been a day that Rose would never forget. In the future she was to travel to the ends of the earth and to learn to think nothing of it, but those few hours in Italy had held an undying magic and strangeness.

"I wish it need never end," said Drina one day, as she and Rose skated hand in hand. It was dark and the ice was illuminated by coloured lights. So far they had skated with various members of the party, but had come together at last.

"So do I," Rose agreed soberly. "Only four more days and then dreary old London again."

"And what wouldn't *I* give to see dreary old London! Think of me, you lucky girl."

"Do you really mind?"

"Dreadfully," Drina said sombrely. "I don't know

how I shall face three more months of it, even with Tamina's company and Miss Selby thinking me better than she imagined at first."

The very next morning, as they finished their coffee in the emptying dining-room, Drina made some remark about returning to Lugano, and Mrs Chester gave her rather an odd look, then glanced at her husband and nodded.

"You tell her, James. It's your pigeon."

Mr Chester looked across at Drina's suddenly anxious face and smiled warmly.

"It's all completely settled, so why not? Put the poor girl out of her misery. You don't want to go back to Lugano, do you, Drina?"

Drina looked blank. Of course she didn't want to go back, but how could she say so?

"What do you mean, Grandfather?"

"You put on a brave face and were very, very good, but you hated it. Now admit it."

Drina was silent.

"You did it for me, and it was splendid of you, but it wasn't right and I never thought so. That was even before I knew about *The Land of Christmas* and refusing the film offer."

"Miss Volonaise told you," said Drina, with a gasp.

"She did, but only because I insisted on knowing. I'm much better, and I shan't worry, neither will your grandmother. It's all finally arranged, after some letters and a few telephone calls that you never knew about. You're going back to the Dominick with Rose."

Drina was absolutely white and Rose, too, looked staggered.

"Oh, Mr Chester –!"

"But, Grandfather –!"

"Miss Selby has been very good about it and isn't

even charging us next term's fees. She's sorry to lose you, in some ways, but she says she realises that you were in the wrong place at her school. She seems most impressed by your talents."

"Glad to get rid of me," said Drina. She glanced helplessly at her grandmother and received an almost imperceptible nod. Mrs Chester looked calm and resigned.

"It's true, Drina," she said. "You're to live with Miss Whiteway and have next term in Red Lion Square. I hope you're pleased?"

Drina had leaped to her feet, her face blazing with delight.

"Really? And it's really all right? Oh, Granny! Grandfather! Oh! Oh!" And she almost danced where she stood, to the amusement of the remaining guests and the young Swiss girls who were starting to clear away.

"Sit down again, Drina. Everyone is looking at you. I'm told that you're perfectly capable of getting yourself and Rose safely back to London, so please try and show some good sense. Your trunk and anything you've left can follow you when we get home to the villa. And, early in April, we'll be back in London. Your grandfather has started to enquire about flats in St John's Wood. I hope you're satisfied?"

"Oh, Granny, yes. So long as it's all right."

"Then you and Rose run away now. You both look as though you'll explode."

Drina and Rose obeyed, dashing up the flights of stairs. Once in their room Drina did a wild dance of joy, until she slipped on the polished floor and fell headlong on to Rose's bed, nearly suffocating in the down covering. She sat up, gasping and scarlet in the face.

"Oh, wonderful, *wonderful*! Oh, bus queues again,

and smelly old cloakrooms and that chain that won't pull! And Igor and Jan and beastly, beastly Queenie and Sylvia! Puddles and rice pudding in the canteen and colds and aching feet!"

They burst into wild laughter and embraced each other suddenly. It was as though they had been given the whole world.

6

Drina and Rose in Danger

Before she and Rose went out Drina managed a few words with her grandfather.

"Are you *sure* it's all right? I did mean to stay until April."

"Yes, it is, I promise you. And your grandmother fully agrees. She admits she was wrong and that she more or less forced you –"

"She didn't entirely. I made up my own mind."

"You're a good girl, but we don't want any more sacrifices. Go back to the Dominick and get on with your real work. I'm bitterly sorry about *The Land of Christmas*. I was as soon as we learned that it was being put on in London and that Rose had got the part that should have been yours. And Miss Volonaise told us that she tried to persuade you to stay and take it."

"Not very hard. She knew I wouldn't change my mind. Oh, it *will* be wonderful to go back, though I shall miss you both when you're far away."

"We'll miss you, but the time will soon pass."

The only thing that saddened Drina a little was the thought of leaving Tamina to spend her last term

without her. That evening she telephoned her friend
and told her the news, and Tamina was most upset.

"Oh, Drina, I shall miss you so! Don't do it! Please
come back!"

"I can't. It really isn't the place for me. I'm terribly,
terribly sorry, Tamina. But we *will* meet again before
very long. You must come and stay with us at the end of
July. I shall look forward to it."

"Me, too," said Tamina sadly. "Oh, dear! I suppose
one must pay for having a famous friend."

"Don't say that. I'm not going to be even a little
famous any more. I'm going to work like anything at my
schoolwork next term and then work harder still as a
Senior Student. The days of my carefree youth are
behind me."

But no one would have thought so during those last
days in Kandersteg, for Drina was in the wildest spirits.
David, having got over the shock of learning that she
was more important than he had supposed, would
hardly let her out of his sight. He was fascinated by her
gaiety and more than a little in love with her. He made
hopeful plans about seeing her again in London,
though, in fact, his home was near Oxford, but he did
not mention his hopes to Drina, which was just as well.
For she thought him nothing more than a rather
bumptious, reasonably attractive boy. A holiday
companion, no more.

"A bad case of puppy love," said Rose shrewdly, on
one occasion.

"Oh, dear! Do you really think so? Why, he tries to
bully me and make me do what he wants."

"That's the poor lad's way. He thinks he's the big
he-man. You do certainly get 'em at your feet!"

"So do you," said Drina, grinning, for Rose had had
her successes.

"But there's only one that you want, isn't there?"

"Grant?" Drina sobered at once. "Yes, but I have no hope. He's older and far away. He'll want to marry some time soon and it won't be me. I'm too young, and my life is planned, anyway. I *have* to be a dancer. Only after that – some day – I might think of marriage, and then it will be too late."

"You'd really put dancing first?" Rose was a little shocked. She, too, wanted passionately to be a dancer, but then she had never fallen in love, only been mildly attracted. In her heart the one who had attracted her most was Igor, but she had few illusions about this. If the egotistic Igor married at all, his wife would probably have a terrible time; in any case he would never ask *her*.

"Yes, I would. I think I have to, for the next four or five years, or I could never live with myself again."

But it was their last full day in Kandersteg and no time for serious conversations. Many people had left the hotel already and gone back to their own countries, but David and Deborah were still there and would be for another week. Their father was a professional photographer, who wanted to take as many pictures as possible of Switzerland under snow.

It was a sunny morning and Drina and Rose had decided to spend their last day by taking a picnic lunch and going for a walk. The snow was hard and crisp and at midday the sun would be quite warm enough for eating a meal out of doors.

David and Deborah, who had rather abandoned ski-ing now that their party had mostly gone, decided to join them. Drina and Rose agreed politely, though both would really have preferred to go on their own.

"We thought of going up to the Gastern Valley," Drina said, "I went once in summer and it was wonderful. It ought to look really stupendous in the snow, almost frightening. I asked, and the road's fairly clear."

They were just ready to leave, with their food and anoraks in little rucksacks, when Frau Braun met them on the steps.

"Take care," she said. "Don't go too far. I do not trust the weather."

"Why, it's glorious!" cried Deborah.

"But the forecast is not so good, and," she added in German, "my bones tell me that it will snow."

Frau Braun had lived all her life in the valley and probably her bones didn't lie. Drina promised that they would watch the sky and not take any risks, and they set off merrily through the village, towards the frowning crags that hemmed the valley in and through which the trains passed on their way to the Rhone Valley. The only other ways out of the valley at this point were the steep track that climbed the Gemmi Pass and the road that climbed not quite so steeply through tunnels to the remote Gasterntal.

This they took, singing as they went, until the climb made them too breathless and the falling Kander made too much noise. The dark tunnels were eerie, but Drina had brought a strong torch in case of need. And when they emerged at last, almost up at the beginning of the Gastern Valley, the River Kander was a terrible torrent that made a deafening thunder and the rocky walls of the Doldenhorn seemed to hang over them. But the sky was still blue and the sun shone on the pure snow of the Balmhorn.

It was a vast scene, a world of awe-inspiring solitude, and it seemed very different from the way it had looked on that summer day of wild strawberries and flowers. Drina remembered clumps of pink alpine crowfoot clinging to the rocks, and little scabious, yellow rock roses, pinks and a host of others growing almost up to the snowline.

"Doesn't anyone live up here?" asked David, awed, in spite of himself, by the white desolation.

"I think only in summer," said Drina. "I fancy they bring the cattle here, and then there are one or two hotels. There's a tiny village a long way towards the glacier. But I don't really think that anyone lives there all the year round."

They ate their lunch on a bank of hard snow, with newspapers and their anoraks under them to keep out the cold, and the sun was so warm that they were able to sit with bare arms.

"Think of London!" said Rose. "Drina, you must be crazy!"

"Maybe," Drina agreed. "Of course I shall miss all this. But I'd be leaving, anyway. No, it's been perfect, but I shall go cheerfully back to dark and cold and rain." And, sitting there on a bank of snow in the lonely Gasterntal, she thought happily of the Dominick and all her friends.

By the time they had packed up their things there were clouds in the sky and a cold wind suddenly blew up the valley. Drina said quickly:

"I think we'd better go back now. The weather changes so quickly in the mountains and Frau Braun said that there'd be snow."

"Oh, not yet," said Deborah impatiently. "Let's go on to the woods. Maybe we could reach that village and see if there's anyone there. She never actually mentioned snow."

"She did, but you don't speak German. It's a long way to the village, and, even without snow, it gets dark early."

"Oh, come on! Quit arguing, you women." David

swung his rucksack on to his shoulders. "It's early to turn back and we may never be here again."

"But if it does snow –" Drina had the deepest respect for the mountains and every instinct told her that it would be folly not to turn towards home now.

"It won't snow till dark. I'm the leader of the party and *I* say it'll be all right."

"Who said you're the leader?" asked Rose, who agreed with Drina. She was suddenly finding the deep, enclosed valley really frightening and longed for the sight of other human beings.

"Well, I'm the only man."

"So what?" Deborah said, laughing. "Still, I'd like to go on. Come on, you others. Be sports. Don't say you're scared?"

"I am, rather," Drina said grimly, but did not resist when David seized her by one arm and Deborah took the other. They set off, almost running, and Rose followed.

"Drina's right. I'm scared, too. I think we should turn back soon. Look at the sky!"

Within ten minutes the sunlight had entirely gone and the sky had a strange yellowish look. The wind blew very coldly indeed and the whole scene was as desolate as the mountains of the moon. Even David was at last daunted, though it went against the grain to admit that he had been wrong.

"Oh, well, better turn back, I suppose. It doesn't look too promising."

"It's snowing already," said Rose, pointing to a few flakes on Drina's dark green anorak.

The few flakes turned, in less than five minutes, into a whirling feathery mass. When they looked back the Balmhorn had quite disappeared and even the nearer rock walls of the Doldenhorn were only dimly

suggested – an unbelievable precipice, ghostly in the snow.

A fresh white covering obscured the narrow road and the strange delta-like land by the river, and the snow was in their faces, so that they lowered their heads and tried to shield their eyes against it. Once David, who was leading, found that he was off the road and heading towards the water, for the Kander flowed more quietly here, before its wild plunge down to the Kander Valley.

Drina and Rose, gripping hands, fought their way onwards in grim silence. They needed all their energy, for the wind was growing fiercer and they had to fight against it, as well as against the heavy flakes. Their hoods covered their ears, but their cheeks felt numb with the cold and sometimes they could hardly see more than a foot or two in front of them.

"We'll be all right when we get to the tunnels!" David shouted back. "Better keep close together."

"There are some horrid drops near the Kander Falls!" Drina shrieked. "Do be careful!"

David and his sister were tall and very strong. Drina was in good condition, but small and slight, and Rose had little real stamina. Besides, she was terrified. A child of the city streets, she had only rarely come up against the full force of the elements. There had certainly been snow during her years in the Chilterns, but it had been gentle compared to this white horror, with the knowledge of vast desolation all around.

Drina was frightened, too, for she had few illusions about the savage danger of winter in the high Alps. If they had turned when she suggested, they would have been almost down in the lower valley by now, where there were hotels and plenty of chalets, even before the village started properly. There would have been no real danger if they had all obeyed the dictates of common sense, and she cursed herself roundly because she had allowed David to over-ride her.

Battling on, with Rose's hand clinging to her wet glove, she thought of the Dominick again and wondered if she would ever walk across Red Lion Square after all. To die in the Alps would be dreadful; to die at sixteen, with all her high hopes coming to nothing.

Frau Braun knew where they had gone, but by the time she grew worried and sent out a search party they might already be buried in a drift. Bodies were sometimes not found until the spring. She had dreadful visions of a tombstone in Kandersteg: "Drina Adams, aged 16. Died in the Gasterntal –"

Rose clutched her more convulsively and said something. Drina stopped and turned to her friend.

"What is it? Are you all right?"

"I don't kn-know. I s-suppose so. Do you think we'll ever make it?"

"Of course we will." Thoughts of the tombstone receded as Drina made an extra spurt, taking Rose with her. "We'll be all right when we start going down."

"Perhaps a d-drift will close one of the tunnels."

"Not yet. Drifts take hours to form." But would they, when the snow was already so heavy and the wind so strong? Suppose a small avalanche closed the road? Suppose –

Drina found that David and Deborah had come back. Their white-covered figures loomed over them.

"–help," she heard David say, and he placed himself between Drina and Rose, holding each by the arm. Suddenly his size was a comfort.

They heard the roar of the falling river well before they reached the place where the narrow road swept round to the mouth of the tunnel, crossing the river by a bridge. Deborah found the bridge and they all made their way cautiously across it, for the surface was slippery with new snow. Now they were sheltered to some extent and the wind was not so fierce. The black entrance to the tunnel loomed up and they hurried towards it.

They huddled in out of the storm and for a few moments it seemed the most wonderful of havens.

7

Back to the Bus Queue

But they had to go on. That was obvious and imperative. David had by now changed from a careless, bumptious boy to a grim-faced young man who realised what he had done and held himself responsible for the rest of the party.

"I'm sorry. I'm really sorry! But we'll make it. Never fear."

Rose, white and exhausted, was the greatest problem, but she revived a little when she had eaten some chocolate.

"I'm all right. Honestly I am. Let's go on."

She confessed afterwards that she, too, had been seeing her grave in Kandersteg churchyard. She had visualised her poor, untravelled parents having to come to Switzerland for her funeral, and had even seen newspaper headlines: "Young Ballet Dancers Dead in Snowstorm."

"And life never seemed so wonderful," she said, as she and Drina lay in bed hugging hot water bottles, after hot soup and lectures from everyone. David and Deborah had taken all the blame, but that hadn't stopped people saying that Drina and Rose should have been firmer in their refusal to go on.

"It was only ten minutes or so," Drina had told her grandmother. "Maybe it wouldn't have made all that much difference. The storm came up so quickly. We were as safe as anything before that, on a perfectly good road in a perfectly flat valley."

"You shouldn't have gone so far in winter. Frau Braun told us that she'd warned you herself. What shall I say to Rose's parents if she's ill again, and all because I trusted you both to be sensible?"

But Rose wasn't ill. She had a good night's sleep and awoke feeling quite all right. It was still snowing, so there was no question of going out. The four young people spent the morning playing records, and, in between whiles, reliving their adventure. David was still extremely contrite.

"I might have deprived the world of a great dancer," he said ruefully. "Two great dancers, I mean."

Drina found that she liked David better than she had done all through the holidays, for he was still subdued and somehow a great deal more adult. But she did not suppose that she would ever see him again, nor greatly wish to do so.

Drina and Rose were to travel to Basle on the six o'clock train. Sleepers had been booked for them on the night train from Basle to Calais, and they were to have a meal in the station restaurant.

Mrs Chester captured Drina after lunch for a last talk.

"You must take great care. Don't leave the station in Basle, and ask a porter to find your sleeping-berths. Make sure you have your passport in a safe place – both of you – and don't lose the tickets."

"Granny," said Drina, with spirit, "I speak four languages, I'm used to travelling and I promise you that we'll be all right.''

''Very clever, I'm sure,'' said Mrs Chester tartly. ''But you're only sixteen for all that, and you never *have* travelled anywhere quite alone, especially overnight. If you're seasick crossing the Channel, one of the stewardesses will look after you.''

''And I've never been seasick in my life.''

''It's not too late to start. The Channel can be nasty in winter. Well,'' her tone softened, ''I suppose I can trust you to be sensible. Miss Whiteway will meet you at Victoria tomorrow and she has promised to telephone us at once. Look after yourself in London, don't work *too* hard, and write often. We'll send all your things, and there's no need to worry about us.''

Mr Chester privately gave Drina a generous amount of money.

''I don't want you to be short during the term, though your grandmother believes that young people don't need much. Of course, if you're stuck, you have your Savings account, or my bank can let you have some money. Take care, love, and enjoy yourself.'' And Drina hugged him wildly, for a moment almost sorry that she was going back to London.

It was dark when they were put on the train by Mr and Mrs Chester, but it had stopped snowing and there was a hint of a moon behind the high peaks. The train rushed off down the valley and began to spiral its way down to the lakeside far below. Rose stood in the corridor, trying to see out.

''I have loved it and I may never come back. I think I want to travel more than anything in the world.''

''You'll travel as a dancer,'' said Drina, standing beside her. Now they were down, and through Spiez, and lights gleamed across the dark waters of the Thunersee.

"I suppose so. If I make it. Maybe I'll dance Giselle at the Bolshoi." And suddenly, strangely, Rose looked transfixed with certainty. "Drina, just for a moment I was *sure* that it would come true."

In that moment Drina had been sure, too, for Rose. For herself she was not nearly so certain. She wanted success so much that it would be unbelievably bitter never quite to reach the heights; to be only the kind of dependable, respected dancer who got good rôles but never quite made the grade into the small world of great ballerinas. Once she had only wanted to be a dancer; now, consciously and with fear, she wanted to be a *great* dancer. And it was such a lot to ask from life, when only one in several thousand …

"Perhaps it will come true for both of us," she said, trying to speak lightly, and then they settled down in the warm, lighted compartment that they had to themselves.

A few days later Drina awoke in Miss Whiteway's flat and realised that it was the first day of term. She leaped out of bed and drew the curtains, revealing the dreary dawn-light and a view of wet pavements and grey roof-tops, with just a glimpse of the towers of Westminster Abbey.

Looking at the scene, she chuckled to herself. London instead of Lugano, where, in a very few weeks, there might be signs of spring.

"But it's what I want," she said aloud, as she put on her warm red housecoat and ran to the bathroom.

In the two or three days she had been in London she had seen some of her friends and already her Swiss life seemed far in the past. She had spoken to Jenny on the telephone, too, and had found that some of the hard cheerfulness had gone out of Jenny's voice. She had sounded softer and much happier. Jenny was engaged to be married and the wedding was planned for the following September, when the old Hogdens were handing over the farm to Robert.

It had been a shock, in spite of Jenny's warnings, and Drina was still not used to the idea.

"I hope you'll be my bridesmaid," Jenny had said. "Or are you too grand for a small country wedding?"

Yes, Drina would be her bridesmaid and would hope with all her heart that her friend was going to be happy.

"I'm not passionately in love," Jenny had written, in a letter that closely followed the telephone call. "I don't think I believe in all that stuff about wild rapture. But Robert and I get on and I think we *need* each other. I'm sober and sensible and I want a home and children and a husband I can share things with. I want the farm, too, but I wouldn't do it just for that."

It might be enough, but Drina *did* believe in wild rapture. She had known it during a few days in New York and Paris: a positive, overwhelming awareness and happiness.

"But Jenny isn't me," she thought, as she dressed in her Dominick uniform. "I'm a romantic, I'm afraid. Anyway, I shall never marry Grant."

An hour later she set off into the cold, raw January world, carrying her case and with her Dominick scarf wound several times round her neck. There were puddles by the bus stop and an icy wind blowing off the river. But her heart was light, for she was going back to her own place. To hard work and some difficulties, of course, but none of that mattered.

The Dominick ... It had to be the Dominick, and she would not be afraid of the future. The bus came and she scrambled for the last seat, hearing the conductor's fretful voice crying:

"Nar then, nar then. We ain't got all day."

They swung off up Whitehall, past the anxious-faced people hurrying to work. And Drina sat clasping her case, remembering her mascot Hansl inside it, who had sat in a number of theatres already. Some day Hansl and hard work might bring her wonderful opportunities again.

DRINA

Follow Drina's fortunes, from her first ballet lessons to her triumphant appearances on stages throughout the world, in the popular Drina series of books.

Ballet for Drina	£2.99 ☐
Drina's Dancing Year	£2.99 ☐
Drina Dances in Exile	£2.99 ☐
Drina Dances in Italy	£2.99 ☐
Drina Dances Again	£2.99 ☐
Drina Dances in New York	£2.99 ☐
Drina Dances in Paris	£2.99 ☐
Drina Dances in Madeira	£2.99 ☐
Drina Dances in Switzerland	£2.99 ☐
Drina Goes on Tour	£2.99 ☐
Drina, Ballerina	£2.99 ☐

All Simon & Schuster Young Books are available at your local bookshop or can be ordered direct from the publisher. Just tick the titles you want and fill in the form below. Prices and availability subject to change without notice.

Simon & Schuster Cash Sales Department, PO Box 11, Falmouth, Cornwall, TR10 9EN, England.

Please enclose a cheque or postal order to the value of the cover price and allow the following for postage and packing:
UK: 80p for the first book, and 20p for each additional book ordered up to a maximum charge of 12.00.
BFPO: 80p for the first book, and 20p for each addition book.
OVERSEAS & EIRE: £1.50 for the first book, £1.00 for the second book, and 30p for each subsequent book.

Name ....

Address ....

....

Postcode ....